# The wise monkey

Hash Blink and Thomas Sheriff

Published by Blink & sheriff Publishing House, 2024.

This is a work of fiction. Similarities to real people, places, or events are entirely coincidental.

THE WISE MONKEY

**First edition. November 8, 2024.**

Copyright © 2024 Hash Blink and Thomas Sheriff.

ISBN: 979-8227550835

Written by Hash Blink and Thomas Sheriff.

# Also by Hash Blink

The wise monkey

# Also by Thomas Sheriff

The wise monkey

# Table of Contents

The wise monkey ................................................................. 1
Chapter 1 ........................................................................... 3
Chapter 2 ........................................................................... 7
Chapter 3 ......................................................................... 11
Chapter 4 ......................................................................... 15
Chapter 5 ......................................................................... 19
Chapter 6 ......................................................................... 23
Chapter 7 ......................................................................... 29
Chapter 8 ......................................................................... 33
Chapter 9 ......................................................................... 37
Chapter 10 ....................................................................... 43
Chapter 11 ....................................................................... 49
Chapter 12 ....................................................................... 53
Chapter 13 ....................................................................... 57
Chapter 14 ....................................................................... 63
Chapter 15 ....................................................................... 69
Chapter 16 ....................................................................... 73
Chapter 17 ....................................................................... 77
Chapter 18 ....................................................................... 81
Chapter 19 ....................................................................... 85
Chapter 20 ....................................................................... 89
Chapter 21 ....................................................................... 93
Chapter 22 ....................................................................... 97
Chapter 23 ..................................................................... 101
Chapter 24 ..................................................................... 105
Chapter 25 ..................................................................... 109
Chapter 26 ..................................................................... 115
Chapter 27 ..................................................................... 119
Chapter 28 ..................................................................... 123
Chapter 29 ..................................................................... 127
Chapter 30 ..................................................................... 131
Chapter 31 ..................................................................... 135
Chapter 32 ..................................................................... 139

Chapter 33 ............................................................................................. 143
Chapter 34 ............................................................................................. 147
Chapter 35 ............................................................................................. 151
Chapter 36 ............................................................................................. 155
Chapter 37 ............................................................................................. 159
Chapter 38 ............................................................................................. 163
Chapter 39 ............................................................................................. 167
Chapter 40 ............................................................................................. 171
Chapter 41 ............................................................................................. 175
Chapter 42 ............................................................................................. 179
Chapter 43 ............................................................................................. 183
Chapter 44 ............................................................................................. 187
Chapter 45 ............................................................................................. 191
Chapter 46 ............................................................................................. 197
Chapter 47 ............................................................................................. 203
Chapter 48 ............................................................................................. 209
Chapter 49 ............................................................................................. 213
Chapter 50 ............................................................................................. 217
Chapter 51 ............................................................................................. 221
Chapter 52 ............................................................................................. 225
Chapter 53 ............................................................................................. 229
Chapter 54 ............................................................................................. 233
Chapter 55 ............................................................................................. 237
Chapter 56 ............................................................................................. 241
Chapter 57 ............................................................................................. 245
Chapter 58 ............................................................................................. 249
Chapter 59 ............................................................................................. 253
Chapter 60 ............................................................................................. 257
Chapter 61 ............................................................................................. 263
Chapter 62 ............................................................................................. 267
Chapter 63 ............................................................................................. 271
Chapter 64 ............................................................................................. 275
Chapter 65 ............................................................................................. 279
Chapter 66 ............................................................................................. 283
Chapter 67 ............................................................................................. 289

|  |  |
|---|---|
| Chapter 68 | 293 |
| Chapter 69 | 297 |
| Chapter 70 | 303 |
| Chapter 71 | 309 |
| Chapter 72 | 315 |
| Chapter 73 | 321 |
| Chapter 74 | 325 |
| Chapter 75 | 329 |
| Chapter 76 | 333 |
| Chapter 77 | 337 |
| Chapter 78 | 343 |
| Chapter 79 | 349 |
| Chapter 80 | 353 |
| Chapter 81 | 357 |
| Chapter 82 | 363 |
| Chapter 83 | 367 |
| Chapter 84 | 373 |
| Chapter 85 | 379 |
| Chapter 86 | 385 |
| Chapter 87 | 389 |
| Chapter 88 | 393 |
| Chapter 89 | 397 |
| Chapter 90 | 401 |
| Chapter 91 | 405 |
| Chapter 92 | 409 |
| Chapter 93 | 413 |
| Chapter 94 | 419 |
| Chapter 95 | 423 |
| Chapter 96 | 427 |
| Chapter 97 | 431 |
| Chapter 98 | 437 |
| Chapter 99 | 441 |
| Chapter 100 | 445 |

# THE WISE MONKEY

A Forest's Last Stand Against Destruction, Adventure, and the Power of Unity.

A novel

## Chapter 1

As the sun began to rise over the dense forest, Ling the wise monkey stretched out his arms and legs, ready for another day of adventure. Ling was small in size but his intellect was mighty. He had spent years learning from the other animals in the forest, gaining knowledge on how to navigate the dense foliage and avoid danger.

Today, Ling had a new mission. He had received word from the birds that there was trouble brewing in the nearby village. The humans were planning to cut down the forest to expand their city, and the animals were at risk of losing their homes.

Ling knew he had to act fast. He scampered through the forest, dodging branches and leaping from tree to tree until he reached the edge of the village. He peered through the bushes and watched as the humans began to set up their equipment.

Ling knew he couldn't take on the humans alone, but he also knew he wasn't completely alone in his mission. He had gathered a group of like-minded animals who shared his passion for the protection of their home. Together, they could stop the humans and save their beloved forest.

Ling let out a loud screech, alerting his animal friends that it was time to take action. They responded with an array of calls and howls, and soon they were all gathered in a circle, discussing their plan.

Ling listened carefully to each animal's suggestion, weighing the pros and cons of each idea. Finally, he had a plan that would ensure their success.

As the sun began to set, Ling and his animal friends crept into the village, ready to execute their plan. They moved with stealth and precision, taking out each human one by one and destroying their equipment.

As they retreated into the forest, Ling knew that they had won this battle, but the war was far from over. The humans would continue to try and take their home unless they banded together and fought for what was rightfully theirs.

Ling knew that his role as the wise monkey was just beginning, and he was ready for whatever obstacles lay ahead.

## Chapter 2

Ling returned to his tree perch, feeling a mix of relief and triumph after their victory over the humans. The forest was safe, at least for now.

But as the days went by, Ling couldn't shake off a sense of unease. He had always been the protector of the forest, but now, the responsibility felt heavier than ever. Ling knew that there was always another danger lurking around the corner, threatening the delicate balance they had fought so hard to maintain.

One morning, as Ling was swinging from branch to branch, he heard a faint cry for help. He followed the sound and found a family of birds huddled together on a branch, their nests on fire. Without hesitation, Ling rushed into action. He gathered his animal friends who were quick to extinguish the flames and rescue the birds.

As they put out the fire, Ling couldn't help but

wonder who could be behind this act of destruction. He knew it was no accident. Someone was deliberately causing harm to the forest, and Ling was determined to find out who.

Gathering his animal allies, Ling organized a meeting at the center of the forest. Birds chirped, squirrels chattered, and butterflies fluttered around, sharing their observations and concerns. It became clear that every corner of the forest was under threat.

Ling stepped forward, his voice filled with determination. "We must act swiftly to protect our home. Together, we can overcome any challenge that comes our way. But we need to discover who is behind these attacks. We must uncover the truth."

His friends nodded in agreement, their eyes reflecting their determination. They understood the magnitude of the task ahead.

Days turned into weeks, as Ling and his companions tirelessly searched for clues. Their search took them deep into the heart of the forest, where they stumbled upon a hidden campsite. Ling's keen eyes immediately recognized the signs of human activity.

Cautiously, they approached the campsite, camouflaging themselves among the thick foliage. There, they discovered a group of loggers, axes in hand, preparing to strike down the trees surrounding them. Ling's heart sank as he realized the scale of the operation.

"We won't let them destroy our home!" Ling whispered fiercely to his friends.

With swift and coordinated movements, Ling and his companions thwarted the loggers' every attempt to harm the forest. The loggers soon realized they were no match for the wise monkey and his allies, retreating hastily from the forest.

Exhausted but relieved, Ling watched as the loggers disappeared. While one battle had been won, he knew the war was not over yet. There would always be those who sought to exploit the forest for their gain, but Ling was ready to face any challenge that came their way.

As the sun began to set, casting a warm glow across the treetops, Ling addressed his fellow animals. "We have shown that we are strong and united. Together, we can protect our home from any threat. Let this be a reminder to all who dare harm our forest. The wise monkey and his friends will always stand guard."

With those words, Ling and his companions stood tall, ready to face whatever challenges would come their way, knowing that they had the strength, wisdom, and determination needed to protect their beloved home.

## Chapter 3

Ling perched high atop his favorite tree, the branches swaying gently beneath him. The victory over the loggers had boosted his confidence, yet his wise eyes remained vigilant. He couldn't help but sense a lurking danger, a shadowy threat that awaited them.

His animal friends gathered around him and shared his unease. They had won the battle, but their war to protect the forest was far from over. Their keen senses picked up on the whispering winds, carrying murmurs of new human plans.

Ling's keen eyes spotted a group of loggers, led by a burly man with a scowl etched onto his face, marching purposefully towards the forest. Their axes glinted menacingly in the sunlight, reflecting the greed that burned within their hearts.

"We won't let them harm our beloved home,"

Ling declared, his voice laced with determination. The animals nodded in agreement, their trust in Ling unwavering.

With silence as their ally, Ling and his animal allies embarked on their mission once again. They moved stealthily through the dense foliage, slipping between the shadows cast by the towering trees. Ling's nimble paws barely made a sound as he led the way.

As they neared the campsite, the animals' hearts thundered in their chests. Would their plan succeed once more? Ling's sharp mind conjured up a strategy, his wisdom guiding their every move. With a flicker of his tail, he signaled his comrades to surround the campsite from all sides.

The loggers, oblivious to the presence of their greatest foe, worked with haste, their axes biting into the bark of innocent trees. Ling's eyes narrowed, fueling his determination to protect all that he held dear.

The animals launched their attack, striking fear into the hearts of the loggers. Squirrels chattered and darted, distracting the humans as Ling's fellow primates swung from tree to tree, snatching the axes from their grasp. Birds swooped down, their sharp beaks pecking at the loggers' heads.

Confusion and chaos reigned within the campsite. Ling seized this moment, appearing before the burly man, his eyes ablaze with an unwavering resolve.

"The forest is not yours to destroy," Ling spoke, his voice commanding attention. "Our home will remain untouched. Leave now and never return."

The loggers, startled and defeated, retreated from the forest, their greed overshadowed by Ling's wisdom and the united front of the animal kingdom.

Ling watched as they disappeared into the distance, a sense of triumph filling his heart. But he knew deep down that their victory was temporary. The humans would return, driven by greed and the desire for profit.

As Ling descended from his perch, his animal friends gathered around him once more. They shared a knowing glance, ready to face the challenges that lay ahead. For as long as Ling, the wise monkey, stood by their side, the forest would forever remain protected.

And so, with unyielding determination in their hearts, they prepared for the battles yet to come, knowing that their unity and wisdom would hold the key to their ultimate victory.

## Chapter 4

The sun rose high in the sky, casting a warm golden glow across the forest. Ling and his animal friends reveled in their recent victories, feeling a renewed sense of hope. They gathered near the river, their laughter and playful chirps filling the air.

Ling swung from tree to tree, his tail swaying with each graceful movement. He couldn't help but notice how the tension that had once weighed heavily on their hearts seemed to dissipate. The forest was breathing easier, its vibrant life energy flowing freely once again.

As Ling perched on a branch, he observed a family of deer grazing peacefully nearby. The gentle creatures no longer had to worry about the menacing chainsaws that had threatened their existence just days before. Ling smiled, grateful for the small victories they had achieved together.

The wise monkey turned his attention to his animal allies, who were joyfully frolicking in the meadow. Cheska, the clever squirrel, scampered playfully, darting in and out of the trees. Oscar, the brave owl, hooted with delight as he soared through the sky, gliding effortlessly on the currents of the wind. And Maya, the swift fox, raced across the meadow, her fur gleaming in the sunlight.

Ling knew that despite the threats that still loomed over their paradise, they needed this moment of respite. The last few battles had taken their toll, both physically and emotionally, but now they could revel in the simple pleasures that the forest offered.

He joined his friends, swinging down from the tree with a graceful leap. The animals gathered around Ling, their eyes shining with gratitude. Ling felt his heart swell with pride. Their unity and unwavering determination had brought them this far, and he knew that together they could conquer any challenge that lay ahead.

As the day drifted into the tranquil evening, Ling and his animal companions sat beneath a majestic oak tree. They shared stories, their voices blending with the rustling leaves and melodic chirps of the forest. Ling listened intently, his wise gaze flickering with a sense of contentment.

The wise monkeys realized that beyond their battles, they had created something truly remarkable. In protecting their home, they had formed an unbreakable bond, a family forged from courage and compassion. Ling felt a warmth in his heart, knowing that they were not alone in this fight.

As night fell and a gentle breeze caressed the forest, Ling looked up at the moon and whispered a silent prayer of gratitude. Despite the uncertainty that still lay ahead, he knew that as long as they stood together, they would always find a way to protect the precious land they called home.

And so, they drifted off to sleep, their dreams filled with visions of a bright and harmonious future. Ling knew that the story of their struggle was far from over, but for this moment, wrapped in the embrace of the forest, they found solace and hope.

## Chapter 5

As the days turned into weeks, Ling and his animal friends continued their vigilant watch over the forest. They patrolled the thick underbrush, always on the lookout for any signs of danger. Ling perched high atop his favorite tree, observed the world below with a wise and watchful eye.

One sunny morning, while Ling was deep in thought, the sound of faint footsteps reached his ears. Alert, he scanned the surroundings, searching for the source of the noise. His heart quickened as he spotted a young girl walking cautiously through the forest.

Ling leaped down from his perch, landing gracefully in front of her. Startled, the girl stumbled backward, almost losing her balance. Ling regarded her with gentle eyes, sensing her fear.

"Do not be afraid," Ling said in a soft,

reassuring voice. "I mean you no harm."

The girl, wide-eyed and trembling, whispered, "I'm lost. I didn't mean to come this deep into the forest."

Ling's compassionate nature took over, and he motioned for the girl to follow him. Guided by his wisdom, he led her through the winding paths, guiding her towards safety.

As they walked, the girl introduced herself as Mei. She explained that she had ventured into the forest out of curiosity, hoping to witness its beauty up close. However, she had underestimated the vastness of the woods and soon found herself disoriented.

Ling listened attentively, understanding her desire to connect with nature. He knew that not all humans were harmful, but caution was necessary. The forest had always provided shelter and peace, and its protection was paramount.

Finally, they reached the outskirts of the forest. Mei stared at Ling, gratitude shining in her eyes. Ling nodded, assuring her that she was safe now.

"Thank you, Ling," Mei murmured. "You saved

me from getting lost forever."

Ling smiled, his wise eyes sparkling with kindness. "Remember, the forest is a delicate balance. We must respect its wonders and protect it from harm."

Mei nodded, promising to carry Ling's message with her always. Ling watched as she retreated, disappearing into the distant landscape.

As Ling returned to his perch, a sense of fulfillment washed over him. Although their encounter had been unexpected, Ling knew that their meeting was a reminder of the forest's importance. Ling understood that sharing their wisdom with humans would be crucial in preserving their enchanted home.

With renewed determination, Ling called upon his animal friends, gathering them together for a meeting. Together, they devised a plan to spread awareness and educate humans about the significance of the forest. Ling knew it wouldn't be easy, but he believed that compassion and knowledge could bridge the gap between both worlds.

And so, Ling and his animal allies embarked on a new mission to protect the forest not only from physical threats but also from ignorance. They would ensure that the wisdom of the wise monkey would touch the hearts of those who needed it most, illuminating their path toward a harmonious coexistence.

The adventure continued, with Ling leading the way, his innate wisdom guiding them through the challenges they would face. With each passing day, Ling's determination grew stronger, fueled by the unwavering belief that they could make a difference.

Little did they know, their journey was far from over. Ling and his animal friends were about to face their greatest challenge yet, one that would test the limits of their courage and the power of their unity. But as always, they stood tall, ready to face the unknown with unwavering hope.

## Chapter 6

As the days turned into weeks, Ling and his animal friends continued their tireless efforts to protect the forest. They patrolled the outskirts, eyes keen and senses alert, ready to defend their home from any potential threat.

One afternoon, Ling sensed a disturbance in the air. He listened intently, his wise monkey ears picking up faint sounds of machinery in the distance. His heart sank as he realized that the loggers were back, their destructive intentions looming over the forest once again.

With a wave of his hand, Ling signaled for his animal allies to gather around him. They formed a tight circle, their eyes filled with determination and resilience. Ling spoke in a hushed voice, "My dear friends, the loggers have returned. We must be prepared for another battle. Our victory over them before was just the beginning."

The animals nodded in agreement, their trust in Ling unwavering. They knew that their strength lay in their unity and the faith they had in one another. Together, they devised a plan to confront the loggers head on, using their unique abilities and instincts to outsmart them.

Under the cover of darkness, Ling and his animal friends approached the loggers' camp. They watched as the flickering glow of the campfire illuminated the loggers' faces, their tools of destruction lying menacingly nearby. Ling's heart filled with anger, but he reminded himself to remain calm and focused.

With a swift movement of his paw, Ling motioned for the attack to begin. The animals unleashed their power, overwhelming the loggers with their speed and agility. Birds swooped down, pecking at exposed flesh, while the squirrels and rabbits nipped at their legs, causing havoc and confusion.

The loggers were caught off guard, stumbled, and fell. Their shouts of surprise mingled with the screeching of the animals, creating a cacophony that echoed through the night. Ling rallied his allies, urging them to keep pushing forward, to never back down.

Despite their best efforts, Ling and his animal friends couldn't help but notice that the loggers had become more organized and determined. They were learning from their past mistakes, adapting to the animals' tactics. It was a sobering realization, but it only fueled their resolve to fight harder, to protect their forest with everything they had.

As dawn broke, the loggers retreated, their defeated faces etched with frustration. Ling and his animal allies, breathless but unyielding, watched them disappear into the distance. Ling knew this battle was won, but the war still raged on.

Gathering his friends around him, Ling spoke softly. "We have shown the loggers the strength of our unity, but we must not become complacent. They will return, and we must be ready. Together, we will continue to defend our home, for as long as it takes."

The animals nodded, their eyes gleaming with determination. Ling's wise words resonated deep within them, strengthening their resolve. With a renewed sense of purpose, they scattered into the forest, prepared to face whatever challenges lay ahead.

Ling remained still for a moment, his gaze fixed on the horizon. The weight of their mission pressed heavily on his small shoulders, but he refused to falter. Ling, the wise monkey, would do whatever it took to protect the forest and all those who called it home.

And so, the battle against the loggers continued, each clash bringing Ling and his animal friends closer to their ultimate goal: a future where the forest remained untouched, thriving with life and magic. Together, they would persevere, their bond unbreakable, their actions fueling the hope that one day, harmony between humans and nature would be restored.

## Chapter 7

Ling and his animal friends continued their tireless efforts to protect the forest. Each day, they patrolled the dense foliage, ever watchful for signs of danger. The loggers had grown more cunning and relentless, making each confrontation more challenging than the last. But Ling remained steadfast, fueled by his determination to safeguard the home he cherished.

As they ventured deeper into the heart of the forest, Ling's keen eyes spied something unusual a mysterious figure lurking amongst the underbrush. Curiosity piqued, he signaled his companions to stay back as he cautiously approached.

"Who goes there?" Ling called out, his voice echoing through the trees.

Slowly, the figure emerged from the shadows. It was a young girl, her wide eyes filled with trepidation. Ling recognized her as Mei, the same girl he had saved not long ago. His heart swelled with empathy, knowing that she had returned to this perilous place.

"Mei!" Ling exclaimed, bounding toward her. "What brings you back to the forest?"

Tears welled up in Mei's eyes as she clutched a crumpled letter in her hands. "Ling, I received this letter from my father. He's one of the loggers, but he regrets his actions. He wants to help save the forest instead."

Ling listened intently, his wise eyes focusing on each word Mei spoke. He understood the complexity of the situation a father torn between his duty and his love for his daughter.

"Mei, we must be cautious," Ling replied, his voice filled with concern. "We cannot let the other loggers know about your father's change of heart. It could jeopardize everything we've fought for."

Mei nodded, wiping away her tears. "I understand, Ling. I won't let them find out."

Together, they devised a plan to protect Mei's father and help him in his newfound quest to turn from destruction to preservation. Ling gathered his animal friends, sharing his knowledge of the loggers' tactics and vulnerabilities. It was clear that their battle had evolved into a war of hearts and minds.

Days turned into weeks as Ling, Mei, and her father worked together secretly, planting seeds of awareness and compassion within the logging camp. They shared stories of the forest's beauty, its significance to countless creatures, and the devastating consequences of its destruction.

Gradually, as the loggers began to see the forest through different eyes, the battle lines blurred. Some started questioning their actions, realizing the impact they were leaving behind. Ling's relentless efforts were beginning to bear fruit.

But amidst this newfound hope, Ling couldn't shake the feeling that something even more significant was at play. There was a hidden force, a shadowy presence that seemed to be orchestrating events from the darkness, determined to obstruct their progress.

As the moon rose high in the night sky, Ling climbed to his tree perch, gazing out over the forest he had fought so fiercely to protect. The unease he had felt, the lingering danger it all pointed towards a formidable foe they were yet to face.

Ling vowed to uncover the truth behind this mysterious adversary, to bring an end to their destructive plans once and for all. With Mei, her father, and his loyal animal companions by his side, Ling prepared to face the ultimate challenge that awaited them.

The wise monkey would not rest until harmony was restored to the forest, and its future secured for generations to come.

## Chapter 8

Ling and Mei stood at the edge of the forest, staring out into the vast unknown. Ling sensed something different in the air, a subtle shift that prickled his fur and sent a shiver down his spine. His keen eyes scanned the horizon, searching for any sign of danger.

As they waited, an unexpected sight caught their attention. A lone figure emerged from the dense foliage, moving with a graceful stride. It was a young woman, her golden hair flowing like sunlight. She wore a tattered cloak, and a glimmer of determination sparkled in her eyes.

Ling leaped down from his perch and approached her cautiously. "Who are you?" he asked, his voice both curious and wary.

The young woman smiled warmly, her eyes twinkling with otherworldly wisdom. "I am Sora," she replied, her voice gentle and soothing. "I have journeyed far to find you,

Ling."

Mei gasped, her eyes widening in surprise. "You know Ling? How is that possible?"

Sora's smile widened. "Ling and I share a connection that stretches beyond time and space," she explained. "I have come to offer my assistance in your fight against the loggers."

Ling exchanged a glance with his animal friends, a mixture of disbelief and hope in their eyes. "Why have you chosen to help us?" he asked, his voice tinged with both gratitude and caution.

Sora reached out a hand, her touch light as a feather, and placed it gently on Ling's head. "The forest is not just your home, Ling," she said softly. "It is a vital part of the balance of nature, and its destruction would have far-reaching consequences."

Ling felt a surge of energy course through his veins as if the forest itself was lending him strength. He looked into Sora's eyes, a newfound determination burning in his heart. "We will fight together then," Ling declared, his voice unwavering. "For the forest, and for all those who call it home."

And so, Ling, Mei, and their newfound ally Sora set out on a new path, united in their purpose. Ling's animal friends gathered around them, their spirits soaring with renewed hope. With Sora's presence, their cause felt stronger than ever before.

As they ventured deeper into the heart of the forest, Ling couldn't shake the feeling that an even greater challenge awaited them. The loggers had become more relentless, their desire for profit blinding them to the forest's true worth. Ling knew that this battle would be the most arduous yet, but he also knew that they were not alone.

Together, they would face whatever challenges lay ahead, drawing strength from the bonds they had formed and the love they shared for their home. Ling, Mei, Sora, and the animals pressed forward, ready to defend the forest with all their might. The echoes of their determination reverberated through the trees, a chorus of unwavering resolve.

Little did they know that their fight had attracted the attention of an even darker force, lurking in the shadows. Ling's instincts whispered of a greater danger on the horizon, one that would test their courage and loyalty in ways they could never have imagined.

But for now, Ling and his allies remained focused, their hearts beating as one, ready to protect the forest they held so dear. They would face the unknown head-on, guided by wisdom, love, and an unyielding spirit.

And so, their journey continued, the wise monkey and his friends embarking on a path that would change their lives forever.

## Chapter 9

The sun shone brightly as Ling, Mei, and Sora ventured deeper into the forest. They walked in a single file, their hearts filled with determination and hope. Ling's eyes darted back and forth, alert for any signs of danger.

Mei skipped ahead, her excitement palpable. "I can't believe we're doing this! We're going to save the forest, right, Ling?"

Ling nodded, a smile tugging at the corners of his mouth. "That's right, Mei. Together, we will protect this forest and all the creatures that call it home."

Sora, with her long braided hair swaying in the wind, added, "And we won't let anything or anyone get in our way."

As they ventured deeper into the forest, Ling noticed the trees standing tall and proud, their branches reaching toward the sky. The rustling leaves whispered stories of resilience and strength. Ling knew that the forest had seen countless battles in its lifetime, but this time, they would emerge victorious.

Their footsteps echoed through the forest, the sound blending with the chirping of the birds and the gentle rustling of the leaves. It was a symphony of nature, a reminder of the harmony they were fighting for.

Suddenly, a distant growl reverberated through the trees. Ling tensed, his muscles coiling like a spring. He held out his hand, signaling his companions to stop. They followed suit, their hearts pounding in anticipation.

Ling motioned towards a nearby tree, urging Mei and Sora to climb up. With the agility of a monkey, Ling leaped onto a branch, blending seamlessly with the foliage.

From their elevated vantage point, they peered through the dense forest. A group of loggers emerged, their chainsaws roaring to life. Mei clutched Sora's hand tightly, her eyes wide with fear.

Ling scanned the area, his mind racing. He knew they needed a plan, a way to deter the loggers without resorting to violence. As he racked his brain for ideas, a sudden thought struck him.

"We have to show them the beauty of this forest," Ling whispered, his voice barely audible.

Mei looked up at him, puzzled. "How? They won't listen to us."

Ling's eyes sparkled with determination. "We'll make them listen, Mei, through art and music."

With that, Ling led Mei and Sora down from the trees. As they approached the loggers, Ling plucked a leaf from a nearby branch and handed it to Mei.

"Play a melody on this leaf, Mei, and let it carry our message."

Mei took the leaf and, with trembling hands, blew across its surface. The leaf transformed into a melodic flute, its sweet sound floating through the air.

The loggers paused, their eyes widening with wonder. Ling stepped forward, his voice steady but resolute. "This forest is home to countless creatures and holds within it a beauty that cannot be replaced. We ask you to see the true value of what you seek to destroy."

Silence enveloped the forest as the loggers pondered Ling's words. Mei's flute continued to play, its gentle music filling the air, touching the hearts of the loggers.

One by one, the loggers lowered their chainsaws, their faces softening with understanding. Ling's plan had worked. Through art and music, they had managed to change their minds.

The forest remained intact, its majesty preserved for future generations. Ling, Mei, and Sora had once again triumphed, not with force, but with the power of their beliefs.

As they walked back through the forest, Ling realized that their fight was far from over. But now, Ling, Mei, Sora, and the loggers would work together, united in their purpose to protect this precious home.

With every step they took, Ling knew that they were writing a new chapter in the story of the wise monkey and their fight to save the forest. And as long as they remained steadfast, Ling believed that their tale would be one of hope, resilience, and the triumph of harmony over destruction.

## Chapter 10

Ling, Mei, and Sora continued their journey through the forest, their happy chatter blending harmoniously with the rustling leaves. The once dense canopy above began to thin, allowing the golden rays of the sun to filter through, illuminating the path ahead. Ling's sharp eyes caught sight of something shimmering in the distance, and his heart skipped a beat.

"Look!" Ling exclaimed, pointing toward a meadow nestled among the trees. "There, beyond the edge of the forest."

Intrigued, Mei and Sora quickened their pace, their curiosity piqued. As they stepped into the meadow, they were greeted by an enchanting sight. A vibrant array of wildflowers bloomed, painting the ground with a mosaic of color. Butterflies and bees flitted about, their delicate wings painting the air in gentle strokes.

"Wow, it's like stepping into a dreamscape," Mei whispered, her voice filled with wonder.

"Nature never ceases to amaze me," Sora added, her eyes shining with appreciation.

Ling nodded in agreement, his eyes scanning

the expanse of the meadow. But as his gaze shifted toward the far end, he noticed a peculiar sight. Dark clouds gathered, swiftly blotting out the sun, and casting an ominous shadow over the meadow.

"Something isn't right," Ling murmured, his voice laced with concern.

As if in response, a rumble of thunder echoed through the air, followed by flashes of lightning that danced across the sky. Raindrops fell lightly at first, tapping a soothing rhythm against the leaves. But soon, the drizzle transformed into a relentless downpour, soaking the meadow within minutes.

"We need to find shelter," Sora shouted over the roaring rain, her face etched with determination.

Ling, Mei, and Sora darted towards a cluster of towering trees, their branches offering a meager shield against the deluge. Huddled close together, they watched as the storm raged around them, the tempest marking its territory with wind and rain.

"This storm feels different, more powerful," Mei said, her voice barely audible above the raging storm.

Ling's eyes narrowed, his mind racing to make sense of the chaotic scene unfolding before them. Could this be the hidden adversary he had sensed? Ling couldn't shake off the feeling that there was more to this storm than mere nature's fury.

Suddenly, a thunderous crack split the air, followed by a piercing cry. Ling's heart sank as he realized the sound had come from the forest. Sweeping Mei and Sora behind him, he dashed towards the disturbance, his agile form navigating through the rain-drenched undergrowth.

There, nestled between two mammoth trees, they found their animal friends shivering, frightened, and soaked to the bone. Ling's heart ached at the sight, as he knew they counted on him to protect them.

"We won't let this storm defeat us," Ling declared, his voice resolute. "Together, we will weather this storm, just as we have faced every challenge before."

With Ling's words igniting a renewed sense of determination, they huddled closer together, their spirits resilient amidst the turmoil. The storm raged on, but within their united circle, they found solace and strength.

As they waited for the storm to pass, Ling couldn't help but wonder if this was the final test they needed to prove the unbreakable bond they shared. Little did they know that this storm was only the beginning of the greatest challenge they would face yet one that would ultimately define their destiny and the fate of the forest they held so dear.

## Chapter 11

The storm raged on, rain pouring down and wind howling through the trees. Ling, Mei, and Sora huddled together under a large, sturdy tree, seeking refuge from the tempest. The animals, too, found shelter beneath the branches, their eyes wide with fear.

As lightning crackled overhead, Ling held onto Mei's hand, his grip comforting and steady. Sora glanced at them, a spark of determination shining in her eyes. "We can't let this storm defeat us," she said, her voice filled with unwavering resolve. "We've faced challenges before, and we'll face this one together."

Mei nodded, her face determined. "You're right, Sora. Ling, remember what our wise monkey always tells us: strength comes not from avoiding storms, but from learning to dance in the rain."

Ling smiled, his eyes reflecting the flickering

light of the storm. "Indeed, my friends. We've come so far, and we can't let a little rain dampen our spirits. We must find a way to bring light into this storm."

As if on cue, a burst of lightning illuminated the forest, revealing a path leading towards a cave hidden amongst the trees. It was as if the forest itself was guiding them to safety.

With renewed hope, they followed the path, stepping carefully over fallen branches and puddles along the way. The storm continued to rage, but their determination pushed them forward. Finally, they reached the entrance of the cave, seeking refuge from the relentless downpour.

Inside the cave, the atmosphere shifted. The air was still and calm, providing a much-needed respite from the chaos outside. Ling, Mei, and Sora found a dry spot to rest, surrounded by the murmurs and rustling of animals seeking shelter alongside them.

As they caught their breath, Ling noticed a flicker of light emanating from the walls of the cave. Curious, he approached, his eyes widening in amazement. The walls were adorned with paintings of vibrant scenes:

animals, trees, and landscapes stretching as far as the eye could see.

Mei joined him, her voice filled with wonder. "Look, Ling! These paintings... they're a celebration of the forest, a reminder of its beauty and the importance of protecting it."

Sora joined them too, her gaze filled with awe. "These paintings hold a power of their own. They remind us why we fight, why we must keep striving to protect this precious place."

At that moment, Ling realized that it was not only the physical strength they possessed that made them powerful. It was their love for the forest, their unwavering determination, and the beauty they saw in the world around them that fueled their fight.

As the storm gradually subsided, they emerged from the cave, hearts lightened and spirits renewed. The rain had washed away their worries and doubts, replaced by a newfound clarity and purpose.

Armed with the beauty of the forest and the strength of their bond, Ling, Mei, and Sora ventured back into the world, replenished with hope. They knew that the next phase of their journey awaited, and they were ready to face it, confident that their love for the forest would guide them toward victory.

And so, they set forth, their steps light and their hearts full, ready to continue their quest to protect the place they called home.

## Chapter 12

In the depths of the cave, Ling, Mei, and Sora sat huddled together, taking shelter from the relentless storm outside. The sound of rain pattering against the cave entrance echoed through the air, and flashes of lightning illuminated the darkness, casting eerie shadows on the walls.

Ling could feel the weight of their mission pressing heavily on his shoulders. The forest was counting on them to be its guardians, its voice in the face of destruction. With each passing moment, Ling's determination grew, his fierce determination to protect the woodland sanctuary burning brighter than ever before.

Mei nestled closer to Ling, her small frame trembling slightly with a mix of fear and excitement. Her eyes sparkled with resilience, mirroring the courageous spirit that had ignited within her since the day she met Ling. Sora, the young woman who had joined their cause, observed their unwavering strength, her resolve strengthening with every passing moment.

As the storm raged on outside, Ling's mind drifted back to the wise words of the ancient forest spirits. He recollected the stories of their resilience, how they had weathered countless storms and emerged stronger than ever.

"We must not lose hope," Ling murmured, his voice barely audible over the storm's fury. "Just as the forest endures, so shall we. Together, we are a force that cannot be broken."

Mei and Sora nodded in agreement, their hearts intertwined with Ling's unwavering determination. At that moment, the bond between them grew stronger, fortified by their shared purpose.

Hours turned to an eternity in the depths of the cave, but eventually, the storm began to subside. The sound of rain faded into a gentle drizzle, and rays of sunlight peeked through the dissipating dark clouds.

With renewed resolve, Ling, Mei, and Sora

emerged from the cave, their eyes filled with newfound determination. The forest awaited their return, calling to them with an urgency that could not be ignored.

Together, they ventured deeper into the woodland sanctuary, their steps guided by an unseen force. Ling could sense the forest rallying behind them, its ancient spirit uniting with theirs. They were not alone in this fight.

As they journeyed further, the forest whispered secrets to them, revealing hidden trails and secret paths known only to its most loyal protectors. Ling, Mei, and Sora followed the guidance of the forest, their spirits lifted by the beauty that surrounded them.

They soon stumbled upon a hidden waterfall, its cascading waters painting a vibrant picture against the lush green backdrop. Ling's eyes sparkled with delight as he watched, knowing that this hidden gem must be preserved for future generations to witness.

Mei and Sora shared in Ling's awe, their hearts swelling with gratitude for the chance to be part of something much greater than themselves. The forest had become their family, its creatures their friends, and they would fight tirelessly to ensure its safety.

As the waterfall's mist enveloped them, Ling, Mei, and Sora stood hand in hand, their hearts united in purpose. They were ready to face whatever challenges lay ahead. With the wisdom of the forest coursing through their veins, they would continue their journey, unrelenting in their quest to protect the precious sanctuary they called home.

The story of Ling the wise monkey and his companions was far from over. The forest's destiny intertwined with theirs, and as they ventured forth, they knew that the true test of their strength and resilience awaited them, just beyond the next bend in the majestic woodland path.

# Chapter 13

As Ling, Mei, and Sora stepped out of the cave, a sense of anticipation hung in the air. The forest seemed quieter than usual, as though holding its breath in anticipation of something unforeseen. Unbeknownst to them, a surprise awaited just beyond the trees.

Ling's keen eyes scanned the surroundings, searching for any sign of trouble. Suddenly, a rustling sound emanated from the shrubs nearby. Ling instinctively gestured for Mei and Sora to stay back, readying himself for whatever lay ahead.

With a swift leap, Ling landed in front of the shrubs, braced for a confrontation. To his astonishment, instead of an enemy, he found himself face-to-face with a group of young children, their eyes wide with wonder.

"Whoa, what are you?" one of the children exclaimed, pointing at Ling's furry physique.

Ling's heart softened as he saw their innocent curiosity. "I am Ling, the wise monkey," he replied, trying to sound as gentle as possible. "What brings you this far into the forest?"

A girl stepped forward, holding out a drawing

of a monkey. "We found your picture in a book about the forest," she said. "We wanted to see if you were real."

Ling couldn't help but smile. "Yes, I am real, just like the beautiful creatures and trees that call this forest their home."

The children gazed at Ling in awe, their eyes flickering with a newfound appreciation for nature. Ling's heart swelled with a sense of purpose - this unexpected encounter was an opportunity to impart his wisdom and inspire a new generation of forest protectors.

"Do you know that this forest is in danger?" Ling asked, his voice filled with concern.

The children shook their heads, their curiosity piqued. Ling proceeded to explain the imminent threat of deforestation, sharing stories of their heroic battles against the loggers.

"We want to help too!" one of the children exclaimed, their eyes shining with determination.

Ling nodded, moved by their eagerness. "Together, we can make a difference. Spread the word about the importance of protecting the forest. Tell your friends, your families, everyone you know."

Excitement and hope radiated from the children as they listened attentively. Ling knew that this unexpected encounter had planted a seed of change within their hearts and minds.

Together, Ling, Mei, Sora, and the newfound group of children ventured deeper into the forest, their mission now even more vital. They sang songs, painted vibrant murals, and shared stories, their actions echoing the beauty and importance of the forest.

As Ling looked at the young faces beaming with determination, he knew that the true power of change lay not just in their own hands, but also in the hearts of those they inspired. With the forest's spirit guiding their footsteps, they pressed on, ready to face the challenges that lay ahead.

Little did they know, a greater test awaited them, one that would require unwavering courage and unity. But for now, they relished in the joy of unexpected encounters and the hope that they had ignited in the younger generation. Together, they were an unstoppable force, bound by their love for the forest and their commitment to protect it.

# Chapter 14

The sun shone brightly through the leafy canopy, casting dappled shadows on the forest floor. Ling, Mei, Sora, and the group of children ventured deeper into the heart of the forest. The children skipped along the moss-covered path, their eyes filled with wonder and excitement.

Ling smiled as he watched the children run ahead, their laughter echoing through the trees. He marveled at their enthusiasm, their genuine desire to protect the home they had come to love. Ling knew that their pure hearts held the key to spreading the message of conservation far and wide.

As they walked, Mei turned to Ling, her eyes shining with determination. "Ling, we've come so far, but there's still much work to be done. How can we be sure that our efforts are making a difference?"

Ling paused, his wise eyes reflecting the flickering light. "Mei, change takes time, but every step we take is important. We have inspired these children and countless others to care for the forest. Together, we can create a movement that will echo through generations."

Sora nodded, her feathers rustling gently in the breeze. "And we must continue educating people about the interconnectedness of all living beings. We must show them that by protecting the forest, we are protecting ourselves."

The group continued their journey, their hearts filled with purpose. Along the way, Ling shared stories of the forest's magical creatures and the harmony they shared with nature. The children listened intently, their eyes widening with each tale.

As they reached a clearing, Ling pointed to a massive tree with gnarled roots stretching deep into the earth. "This is the ancient Oak of Wisdom," he said, his voice filled with reverence. "It has witnessed the birth and growth of this forest, and it holds the secrets and wisdom of nature within its ancient core."

The children approached the tree in awe, their small hands touching its rough bark. Ling placed his hand on the trunk, closing his eyes and connecting with its ancient energy.

A whispering breeze caressed their faces, carrying a message from the forest's spirit. It spoke of unity, the power of collective action, and the importance of preserving the delicate balance of nature.

The children, their eyes shining with newfound determination, formed a circle around Ling and the ancient Oak. They pledged to become stewards of the forest, to spread the message of conservation to their families, friends, and communities.

Ling gazed at each child, seeing the spark of hope and responsibility in their eyes. "Remember," he said softly, "it is not just our duty to protect the forest; it is our privilege. We are the guardians of this sanctuary, and together, we can make a difference."

The children nodded, their young faces filled with conviction. Ling knew that the forest's future was in good hands. With their unwavering spirit and the wisdom of the ancient Oak, they would continue the fight to protect their beloved home.

As the sun began to set over the horizon, casting a golden glow across the forest, Ling, Mei, Sora, and the group of children walked hand in hand, ready to face the challenges ahead. With hearts full of hope and a renewed sense of purpose, they would continue their mission, protecting the forest and all its inhabitants with an unwavering resolve.

For as long as the leaves rustled in the wind and the rivers flowed with crystal-clear water, Ling and his allies would fight to preserve the beauty and magic of their sanctuary. The journey was far from over, and the wise monkey knew that as long as they stood together, they could overcome any obstacle that threatened their home.

With each step, they forged a path towards a future where humans and nature lived in harmony, where the forest flourished, and where the wisdom of the wise monkey would be remembered for generations to come.

## Chapter 15

The wise monkey, Ling, and his loyal companions, Mei, Sora, and the group of children, embarked on a new adventure deep within the heart of the forest. Guided by the whispers of the wind and the rustling leaves, they followed a hidden path that seemed to have been carved out just for them.

As they walked, the children marveled at the vibrant colors of the flowers and the gentle melodies of the birds. Ling smiled, knowing that their appreciation for nature was growing with each step they took.

Suddenly, they stumbled upon a sacred grove, a place where ancient trees reached toward the sky, their branches intertwining like fingers. The air was thick with magic as if they had entered a different realm.

In the center of the grove, a majestic waterfall cascaded down into a crystal-clear pool, creating a symphony of harmonious sounds. Ling's heart swelled with joy, recognizing the significance of this place.

"This, my friends, is the heart of the forest," Ling said, his voice filled with reverence. "It is here that the spirits of the forest reside, watching over all living creatures and nurturing the balance of nature."

The children gazed in awe, their eyes wide with wonder. They understood the privilege of being in this sacred space and the responsibility they had to protect it.

Ling continued, his voice carrying a sense of urgency. "The forest is not just a home for animals and plants. It is a sanctuary, a place of healing and renewal for everyone who seeks solace within its embrace. We must do everything in our power to safeguard it."

The children nodded, their young faces filled with determination. They had seen the destruction caused by careless human activities and were motivated to make a difference.

Together, Ling, Mei, Sora, and the children formed a circle, their hands clasped tightly. They closed their eyes and whispered a promise to the forest, pledging their unwavering commitment to its protection.

At that moment, the ground beneath their feet trembled, and a soft glow enveloped them. It was the forest's spirit, acknowledging their vow and granting them the strength to carry on.

From that day forward, Ling and his allies, along with the children, dedicated themselves to educating others about the importance of preserving the forest. They organized workshops, planted trees, and spread awareness about sustainable practices.

Their efforts gained momentum, and soon people from all walks of life joined their cause. Ling's message of conservation echoed far and wide, reaching the hearts of those who had once turned a blind eye to the forest's plight.

As the sun began to set, casting a warm golden glow over the grove, Ling knew that their mission was far from over. But he also knew that they had kindled a flame, a flickering hope that would endure, no matter the challenges they faced.

With renewed purpose and a growing army of passionate advocates, Ling and his companions stood tall, ready to face whatever lay ahead. For they understood that the forest's survival depended not only on their efforts but on the collective strength of all who loved and cherished it.

And so, with hearts brimming with determination, they set forth, united by a shared vision to protect and preserve the wise monkey's beloved home, the forest, for generations to come.

## Chapter 16

As they journeyed deeper into the forest, the air became lighter and filled with the sweet fragrance of blooming flowers. Ling, Mei, Sora, and the children marveled at the vibrant colors surrounding them, their hearts brimming with joy.

Every step they took seemed to bring them closer to the heart of the forest, where an enchanting meadow unfolded before their eyes. Sunlight danced through the trees, casting an ethereal glow on the grassy expanse.

Ling led the group to a clearing, where they found a sparkling stream meandering through the meadow. The water glistened as it flowed, inviting them to dip their weary hands and quench their thirst.

The children's laughter echoed through the trees, blending harmoniously with the songs of the birds above. Mei's eyes twinkled with happiness as she watched the children chase butterflies, their small feet barely making a sound on the soft ground.

Taking a moment to catch their breath, Ling gazed at the delighted faces around him. He felt a sense of accomplishment, knowing that he had inspired these young hearts to care for the forest. Ling shared a gentle smile with Mei, grateful for her unwavering support.

Sora perched on a tree branch nearby, his golden feathers shimmering in the sunlight. He preened himself with pride, knowing how far they had come in their mission. The forest had become a place of hope, where every small action mattered.

As the day unfolded, Ling and his allies continued their exploration of the meadow, discovering new wonders at every turn. They encountered a family of deer grazing peacefully, their graceful movements mesmerizing the children.

With each passing moment, Ling's heart swelled with gratitude for the beauty and resilience of the forest. He knew that their journey was not over, but for now, they could revel in the tranquility and abundance surrounding them.

As twilight approached, casting a warm golden hue across the meadow, Ling called the children together. He shared stories of the forest's inhabitants, teaching them the importance of respecting and conserving nature.

The children listened attentively, their eyes widening with wonder and understanding. Ling's words resonated deeply within them, planting seeds of compassion and empathy that would blossom into actions.

As the group settled down for the night under a star-filled sky, Ling felt a sense of contentment wash over him. The forest whispered its gratitude, the rustling leaves a chorus of appreciation for their dedication.

In their dreams, Ling, Mei, Sora, and the children saw a future where humans and nature coexisted harmoniously. They envisioned a world where every decision was made with the well-being of the forest in mind.

With renewed spirits, they awoke as the sun began to peek over the horizon, its warmth spreading a golden glow across the meadow.

Ling knew that their journey was far from over, but at this moment, they allowed themselves to simply be present and soak in the magic of the forest.

As they resumed their expedition, Ling, Mei, Sora, and the children carried with them a sense of hope and an unwavering belief in the power of their mission. The forest had touched their souls, igniting a passion that would guide their actions as they continued to protect and preserve their beloved sanctuary.

## Chapter 17

In the depths of the forest, a foreboding shadow loomed, casting a chill over Ling, Mei, Sora, and the children. Ling's keen senses tingled, alerting him to the presence of danger. With furrowed brows and hearts heavy with worry, they pressed on, their steps cautious and measured.

As the group ventured further, the once-vibrant colors of the forest seemed to dim. The once lush foliage now hung low, its leaves wilting and lifeless. Ling's heart sank; he knew that a formidable force was at work, threatening the balance of this sacred sanctuary.

Suddenly, they stumbled upon a clearing, but what they saw within froze them in their tracks. The sacred grove, once teeming with life, now lay in ruins. Trees were felled, their ancient trunks scattered in disarray. Lush vegetation was replaced by the stench of destruction, leaving Ling and his allies gasping for breath.

A gnawing sense of sorrow and anger swelled within Ling's chest as he beheld the devastation. Mei's eyes brimmed with tears, mirroring the pain etched on each face of the children. Sora's wings drooped, burdened by the weight of the desecration before them.

Ling's mind raced, searching for answers. Who could have perpetrated this grievous act? Who could be so blind to the irreplaceable beauty of the forest? Determination surged through his veins, mingling with the anger that fueled his resolve.

Gathering his companions together, Ling spoke with a voice filled with steely resolve. "We must find those responsible for this atrocity and hold them accountable. Our mission to protect the forest takes on a greater urgency now."

The children nodded, their young faces etched with newfound determination. Mei wiped away her tears, steeling herself for the battle that lay ahead. Sora's feathers rustled as he spread his wings, ready to soar to their aid.

With a renewed sense of purpose, Ling and his allies ventured deeper into the forest, following a trail of destruction that wound its way through the ancient trees. Their steps were now fueled by anger and a burning desire for justice.

They knew that the path ahead would not be easy, but they pressed on, their hearts aflame with the belief that they could restore the forest's beauty and protect it from further harm. Ling, Mei, Sora, and the children braced themselves for the battles that awaited them, ready to face the darkness head-on.

Little did they know, their journey would lead them to discover the true scope of their enemy's power. Ling's wisdom, Mei's determination, Sora's loyalty, and the children's unwavering spirit would be put to the ultimate test, as they faced challenges that would shape their destiny and the fate of the forest they held so dear.

## Chapter 18

Ling, Mei, Sora, and the children stood amid the devastated clearing, their hearts heavy with sorrow. The once lush and vibrant forest now lay wounded, its trees felled and its animal inhabitants displaced. Ling's wise eyes filled with determination as he whispered, "We must find those responsible for this destruction and put an end to it."

With renewed purpose, they followed the trail of destruction, expertly reading the signs left behind. The broken branches and crushed foliage led them deeper into the heart of the forest, where the air grew thick with a sense of impending danger. They moved quietly, their senses heightened, seeking any clue that would lead them to the culprits.

As they ventured further, they came across a small cave hidden among the trees. Ling motioned for the group to approach cautiously, warning them of the unknown dangers that might lie within. With steady steps, they entered the dimly lit cavern, their breaths hushed with anticipation.

Inside the cave, they discovered a makeshift campsite. Empty food containers, discarded tools, and the scent of smoke lingered in the air. Mei's nose twitched, and she recognized the scent of the loggers who had previously threatened the forest. Anger welled up within her, fueling her determination to bring justice to her home.

Moments later, they heard a rustling sound coming from deeper within the cave. Ling motioned for everyone to hide, their bodies blending into the shadows as they waited.

Out from the darkness emerged a group of loggers, their clothes smeared with dirt and their faces etched with determination. Their leader, a burly man with a menacing scowl, barked orders to his companions. "We need more wood! Cut down every tree in this forest if you have to!"

The children gasped, their innocent eyes widening in disbelief. Sensing their fear, Sora placed a comforting hand on their shoulders, silently urging them to stay strong.

Ling's eyes narrowed as he observed the loggers, his mind working swiftly to devise a plan. Mei's tail twitched with anticipation, her instincts honed by years of survival in the wild. Sora, too, felt a fire burning within her, fueled by her connection to nature and her unwavering commitment to protecting it.

As the loggers prepared to resume their destructive work, Ling, Mei, Sora, and the children sprang into action. With a swift signal, Ling called forth the forest's allies, rallying the animals to help in their fight.

Birds swooped down, startling the loggers with their sharp beaks and piercing cries. Squirrels scurried around, snatching away tools and creating chaos. The wind howled, stirring the fallen leaves and causing the loggers to stumble. Ling, Mei, Sora, and the children darted in the confusion, sabotaging the loggers' efforts at every turn.

Amid the chaos, Ling's voice resonated, commanding attention. "This forest is not yours to destroy! Its beauty and life are valuable beyond measure. We will protect it with all our might!"

The loggers, overwhelmed and outnumbered, retreated in defeat. Ling, Mei, Sora, and the children stood together, their spirits triumphant. Ling's wise eyes shimmered with pride as he looked at his allies, grateful for their unwavering dedication to their cause.

As the forest settled into a peaceful silence, Ling, Mei, Sora, and the children shared a sense of accomplishment. They knew the journey to protect the forest was far from over, but with each victory, they grew stronger in their resolve.

With the light of a new day dawning, Ling, Mei, Sora, and the children emerged from the cave, ready to face whatever challenges lay ahead. They knew that as long as they stood united, with wisdom, courage, and love for their home, they would continue to defend and preserve the sacred sanctuary they held dear.

Together, they ventured back into the depths of the forest, their hearts filled with hope, vowing to spread awareness and inspire others to protect and cherish the natural world. For in their eyes, the wisdom of the wise monkey shone brightly, guiding their purpose and lighting the way for a future where harmony between humans and nature could flourish.

## Chapter 19

As the sun rose above the forest canopy, Ling, Mei, Sora, and the children gathered around a campfire, their faces illuminated by the dancing flames. They had been traveling deeper into the heart of the forest for days, driven by their unwavering determination to restore its vitality.

Ling sat perched on a fallen tree trunk, his wise eyes surveying the group. He knew that their journey was far from over. The task at hand required more than just their physical presence; it demanded their unwavering dedication and resilience.

"The forest is calling for our help," Ling said, breaking the silence that enveloped the group. "We must find a way to heal its wounds and restore the balance that has been disrupted."

Sora nodded, her eyes filled with a mix of determination and compassion. "We can't give up. Our mission is not just about protecting this forest; it's about preserving the home of countless creatures who depend on it."

Mei, ever the voice of reason, spoke up. "But how do we begin, wise Ling? The devastation is vast, and the path to recovery seems daunting."

Ling's gaze shifted to the children, who sat huddled together, their innocent faces reflecting their concern. He smiled gently, understanding the weight of their burden. "We start by planting the seeds of hope," he said. "We gather the fallen acorns and saplings and nurture them with love and care. Together, we shall grow a new generation of trees, a symbol of resilience and rebirth."

Excitement filled the air as they all rose to their feet, eager to embark on this critical mission. The children clutched small shovels and bags, ready to collect the acorns that would be the foundation of their forest's revival.

As they walked through the forest, Ling shared his wisdom. "Nature has its way of healing itself, but we can aid its recovery by spreading awareness. We must reach out to the surrounding communities and educate them about the importance of preserving our natural treasures."

Mei's eyes sparkled with newfound purpose. "We can organize workshops, create posters, and share stories about the forest's magical wonders. By fostering a sense of connection and understanding, we can ignite a passion for conservation in the hearts of others."

Sora's voice resonated with determination. "We will not rest until the forest thrives once more until it echoes with the songs of birds, rustling leaves, and laughter."

They began their work, digging small holes and gently planting the acorns, their hands brushing against the Earth with reverence. The children followed suit, their eyes shining with the hope of a brighter future.

Days turned into weeks, and their efforts were rewarded with the first sprouts breaking through the ground. A sense of fulfillment filled their hearts as they witnessed the forest's gradual recovery, one tree at a time.

Ling, Mei, Sora, and the children knew there was still much work to be done. But each new leaf, each new bud, reminded them that their united efforts were making a difference.

As the moon cast its gentle glow upon their

camp, Ling spoke with a voice filled with hope. "We may be just a few, but our dedication can inspire others to join our cause. Together, we can protect not just this forest, but all the precious havens of nature."

And so, they continued their journey, guided by Ling's wise counsel and fueled by their unwavering determination. Ling, Mei, Sora, and the children would face the challenges that lay ahead, for they knew that the forest's survival depended on their unwavering commitment.

## Chapter 20

In the heart of the forest, Ling, Mei, Sora, and the children woke up to the gentle rustling of leaves in the morning breeze. They stretched their limbs and shared a hearty breakfast, feeling a renewed sense of purpose.

As they continued their journey, they stumbled upon a hidden waterfall cascading down moss-covered rocks. Its soothing sounds echoed through the trees, captivating their senses. Ling sensed that there was more to this enchanting place than met the eye.

Curiosity piqued, they decided to explore further, navigating through thick underbrush and climbing over fallen branches. A sense of wonder enveloped them as they entered a hidden grove bathed in dappled sunlight.

In the center of the grove stood a majestic ancient tree, its branches reaching toward the sky as if seeking solace. Ling approached the tree, feeling a deep connection with its age-old wisdom.

With a gentle touch, Ling closed his eyes and listened to the whispers of the forest. The tree, pulsating with life, shared its secrets. It spoke of balance, harmony, and the delicate dance between nature and humanity.

As Ling reopened his eyes, he saw the others gathered around him, their faces filled with awe and anticipation. Ling knew that the tree had bestowed upon him a great responsibility.

"Listen, my friends," Ling began, his voice steady and filled with purpose. "This tree has given us a message, a calling to protect not only this forest but every forest beyond its borders. We must share the knowledge we have gained, inspire others, and ignite a global movement to save our planet."

Mei, Sora, and the children nodded in agreement, their hearts aligned with Ling's vision. They understood that the lessons they had learned were not meant to be kept hidden within the confines of the forest but to be shared with the world.

And so, as they embarked on their journey

once more, Ling, Mei, Sora, and the children became ambassadors of change. They traveled far and wide, spreading stories of their adventures, speaking at conferences, and organizing grassroots movements.

Their words touched hearts and minds, awakening a collective consciousness. People from all walks of life united under the banner of conservation, realizing that the fate of the forests and all living creatures rested in their hands.

Through the power of their stories, Ling, Mei, Sora, and the children inspired countless individuals to make a difference, to protect and preserve the natural beauty of the world. They witnessed communities coming together, reclaiming degraded lands, and nurturing them back to life.

The forest, no longer an isolated refuge, became a symbol of hope and resilience, thriving once more as the seeds of compassion and empathy sprouted and flourished.

As the journey continued, Ling, Mei, Sora, and the children understood that their mission was far from over. There were still challenges to face, obstacles to overcome, and new adventures waiting on the horizon.

But armed with their newfound knowledge, unwavering determination, and the wisdom of the ancient tree, they were ready to face whatever lay ahead. Together, they would protect the forests, the creatures that called them home, and the fragile balance of the natural world.

For deep within their hearts, they knew that as long as their voices echoed and their actions inspired, the wise monkey's legacy would continue to guide their path toward a brighter future.

## Chapter 21

Ling, Mei, Sora, and the children ventured deeper into the forest, their steps cautious and hearts heavy with a newfound darkness. The once vibrant foliage now appeared sickly, its leaves dulled and drooping. The air grew thick with an eerie silence, devoid of the usual rustling of animals.

As they pressed on, a heavy fog rolled in, obscuring their vision and concealing the path ahead. Ling's instincts told him that danger lurked in the mist, but he couldn't shake off the feeling of an impending threat.

Through the oppressive haze, they stumbled upon a dilapidated shack a haunting reminder of the encroaching destruction. Blackened trees surrounded the area, their gnarled branches reaching out like skeletal fingers. Ling's heart sank as he realized the shack was a hideout for the loggers, the very ones they had driven away before.

Gathering their resolve, Ling and his companions approached the decrepit structure. The door creaked open, revealing a scene of devastation inside. Tools of destruction lay strewn about, their edges stained with the forest's lifeblood.

Suddenly, a low growl reverberated from the shadows. Ling's eyes narrowed, and he motioned for the others to stay back. With a swift leap, he perched upon a perch, ready to face whatever lurked within.

From the darkness emerged a massive creature a fearsome bear whose once lush fur now hung in patchy tatters. Its amber eyes gleamed with hunger and resentment, a reflection of the pain inflicted upon the forest.

The bear's voice was laced with sorrow as it spoke to Ling, recounting the atrocities it had witnessed. The loggers had not only destroyed the trees but had captured and abused innocent animals, leaving a trail of despair in their wake. Ling's heart ached, knowing he couldn't undo the past, but he could fight for a better future.

Unyielding, Ling addressed the bear with

words of compassion and unity. He knew that change started with healing wounds, bridging the gap between humans and animals. With Mei, Sora, and the children standing beside him, Ling proposed a plan to restore the forest's glory, one voice at a time.

Together, Ling and his unlikely allies set off on a mission to find the loggers, not to punish them, but to educate and enlighten them. They journeyed through the lingering mist, following the tracks left behind by the relentless destroyers.

As they ventured deeper into the heart of darkness, Ling couldn't help but wonder if their message of hope and redemption would be enough to quell the ever-growing greed that tarnished the world.

With each step, the forest echoed with their determination, a symphony of footsteps resolute in their plight. Ling knew that their journey was far from over, and there were battles yet to be fought. But amid the encroaching shadows, Ling and his companions held onto hope, determined to illuminate the way toward a brighter future for the wise monkey and all the creatures that called the forest home.

## Chapter 22

Ling, Mei, Sora, and the children stood frozen in fear as the massive bear loomed before them. Its fur was matted and dirty, a reflection of the sickness that plagued the forest. The bear's eyes were filled with pain, but there was also an undeniable anger burning within them.

Ling took a deep breath, drawing upon the wisdom he had acquired throughout their journey. "We cannot let fear control us," he said, his voice steady. "This bear, like the forest, is suffering. We must find a way to help."

Mei stepped forward, her heart pounding in her chest. "We cannot let this bear harm us or our friends," she said, her voice filled with determination. "But we also cannot harm it. We must find a way to communicate, to show it that we mean no harm."

Sora nodded, his hands trembling slightly. "We've faced many challenges together," he said, his voice wavering. "And we've always found a way to overcome. We can't give up now."

The children mustered their courage, standing alongside Ling, Mei, and Sora, ready to face whatever was to come. They knew that it would take more than physical strength to win this battle. It would require empathy and understanding.

Slowly, Ling approached the bear, his movements gentle and cautious. With every step, he radiated a sense of calmness, hoping to convey his peaceful intentions. The bear growled, its large claws swiping at the ground. Ling stopped, but he did not retreat.

Using the language of the forest, Ling spoke softly, his words carrying the weight of sincerity. "We are not your enemies," he said, his voice carrying through the air. "We are here to heal the forest, to save our home. Please, let us help you."

As if pondering Ling's words, the bear lowered its head and took a step back, its growls subsiding. Ling continued to approach, his hand outstretched, an offering of friendship.

With great caution, he gently placed a paw on the bear's nose. The bear's eyes softened, and for a moment, it seemed as if a spark of recognition flickered within its gaze.

Ling knew that the battle was not over, but a seed of hope had been planted. He turned to his friends, a smile touching his lips. "We have made a connection," he whispered. "Now, we must find a way to heal the forest and this magnificent creature."

Together, Ling, Mei, Sora, and the children devised a plan. They would gather healing herbs and plants from the forest, creating a potion that could alleviate the bear's suffering. But they also knew that the forest needed their help too. They would restore its balance, allowing it to thrive once more.

As they set out on their mission, Ling felt a renewed sense of purpose. The battle against the loggers was only the beginning. Now, they faced an even greater challenge: restoring harmony and healing the wounds inflicted upon the forest and its inhabitants.

With unwavering determination, Ling and his companions moved forward, ready to face whatever obstacles lay ahead. They knew that this journey was not just about saving their home but also about inspiring others to protect and cherish the beauty of nature.

And so, their adventure continued, each step bringing them closer to the ultimate goal: a forest restored, a bear healed, and a world transformed by the power of compassion and love.

## Chapter 23

Ling, Mei, Sora, and the children pressed on, their hearts filled with determination and a sense of purpose. The forest's stillness weighed heavily upon them, as if it held its breath, waiting for their next move. They treaded cautiously through the dense undergrowth, their senses alert and their minds focused.

As they ventured further into the forest, they noticed the signs of destruction left behind by the loggers. Trees lay uprooted, their once vibrant foliage now wilted and lifeless. Ling's heart ached, but he knew they had to press on. They needed to find the source of this sickness and heal it.

Through tangled branches and thorny vines, they stumbled upon a clearing. A hollow emptiness settled within their chests as they beheld the lifeless landscape before them. The ground was barren, devoid of any signs of life.

Not a single blade of grass or the chirp of a bird could be heard. Ling's eyes misted with sadness, yet his resolve remained unshaken.

He beckoned Mei, Sora, and the children to gather around. "We cannot let this devastation consume us," Ling said, his voice steady but filled with determination. "We must be the voice for this forest, a beacon of hope amidst this darkness. Now, let us bring life to this desolate land."

They nodded in agreement, understanding the weight of their task. With shovels in hand, they began to dig small holes in the soil, tenderly planting the saplings they had brought with them. Each one represented a new beginning, a chance to revive the once vibrant ecosystem that had been stripped away.

As they worked, Ling shared stories of the forest's magnificence, the harmony of its inhabitants, and the delicate balance that had been disrupted. The children listened with wide eyes, their hearts brimming with eagerness to make a difference.

Days turned into weeks, and weeks into months. Ling, Mei, Sora, and the children returned to check on the saplings, their faces glowing with anticipation. What they discovered astounded them. The once barren ground now sprouted with vibrant green shoots. The trills of birds filled the air, joining in a joyous chorus of life.

The forest, rejuvenated by their care and dedication, began to thrive once more. Word of their efforts spread like wildfire, igniting a passion for conservation in others. Soon, people from far and wide flocked to the forest, eager to witness the beauty that had been resurrected.

Ling, Mei, Sora, and the children stood amidst the forest's renewed splendor, their hearts swelling with pride. They had become ambassadors of nature, spreading the message of hope and inspiring others to protect and cherish the world around them.

But Ling knew their mission was far from over. The forest still faced many challenges, and there were others like the bear they had encountered before, who needed healing and understanding. Ling's eyes gleamed with unwavering determination.

"We shall continue to protect the forests and all the creatures that call them home," Ling declared, his voice carrying through the rustling leaves. "Together, we can restore what was lost and safeguard the treasures of our world. We are the guardians of this earth, and we shall never falter in our duty."

And so, Ling, Mei, Sora, and the children set forth, their journey far from its end. With each step, they carried the spirit of compassion and resilience, leaving behind a trail of restoration in their wake. For in their hearts, they knew that as long as there was love and determination, the forest would forever thrive.

## Chapter 24

Ling, Mei, Sora, and the children continued their journey through the revived forest, their hearts filled with hope and determination. As they walked, the sunlight filtered through the lush canopy, casting a warm and gentle glow on their path.

With every step they took, they noticed the vibrant colors of wildflowers blooming along the forest floor. Butterflies danced gracefully in the air, their delicate wings carrying them from one blossom to another. The melodious songs of birds filled the air, creating a symphony that lifted the spirits of all who heard it.

The once-sickly trees now stood tall and strong, their branches reaching toward the heavens with newfound vitality. Beams of sunlight filtered through the leaves, creating a magical dance of light and shadow on the forest floor.

Ling led the group to a clearing, where a

breathtaking sight awaited them. A meadow stretched out before their eyes, dotted with wildflowers of every color. The air was filled with the sweet scent of blossoms, inviting them to breathe deeply and savor the tranquility that surrounded them.

As they explored further, they stumbled upon a sparkling stream that wound its way through the forest. The water glistened under the sunlight, beckoning them to dip their hands into its cool embrace. Ling, Mei, Sora, and the children cupped their palms and drank from the stream, feeling refreshed and rejuvenated.

They laughed and played, their worries and fears momentarily lifted from their shoulders. Ling swung from tree branches, Mei danced in the sunlight, and Sora chased butterflies with the children. The forest embraced their joy, joining in their laughter and filling their hearts with an overwhelming sense of peace.

As the day drew to a close, Ling gathered everyone together. They formed a circle, holding hands tightly, and closed their eyes. Ling's voice resonated through the forest, his words carrying a deep sense of gratitude.

"Thank you, dear forest, for your strength and

resilience. We are forever grateful for the beauty and love you have shown us. We promise to protect you with all our hearts, for you are our home."

A soft breeze rustled through the leaves as if the forest was responding to Ling's words. It whispered secrets of its ancient wisdom, assuring them that their efforts were not in vain.

With renewed determination, they walked hand in hand, continuing their journey through the forest. Ling, Mei, Sora, and the children knew that challenges and obstacles may come their way, but they were filled with unwavering hope.

For they had witnessed the miracles that could be achieved when hearts are united in a common purpose. And they were determined to spread their stories far and wide, inspiring others to cherish and protect the wonder of nature.

With each step they took, the forest whispered its gratitude, and in return, they whispered back promises of love and protection. Ling, Mei, Sora, and the children ventured deeper into the forest, ready to face whatever awaited them, knowing that together, they could make a difference and create a future where nature flourished and thrived.

## Chapter 25

As Ling, Mei, Sora, and the children journeyed through the forest, they stumbled upon an unexpected sight. In a clearing ahead, a meadow bathed in the golden glow of sunlight beckoned them forward. The air hummed with an enchanting melody, and colorful butterflies danced in a swirling ballet.

Curiosity tugged at Ling's heart, urging him to explore this newfound paradise. The group approached cautiously, their eyes widening in awe as they stepped into the meadow. The grass beneath their feet seemed to pulse with life, responding to their presence.

In the heart of the meadow, a sparkling stream meandered, its crystal-clear waters inviting them to dip their fingers. Ling led the way, kneeling to cup his hands and take a sip. The water tasted pure and revitalizing, infusing him with newfound energy.

Mei, Sora, and the children joined Ling, their gazes locked onto a mesmerizing sight. Amidst the shimmering stream, fish darted playfully, their scales reflecting the vibrant hues of the forest. Ling couldn't help but smile, realizing the healing power their efforts had unleashed upon this once-sickly land.

As they delved deeper into the meadow, Ling's keen eyes caught a movement in the corner of his vision. Turning his head, he gasped at the sight of a majestic deer, its antlers adorned with blooming flowers. The creature regarded them with intelligent eyes, radiating a gentle wisdom.

"In this enchanted glade," the deer spoke, its voice melodic and soothing, "nature has rewarded your dedication. You have revived the forest, and it has responded with renewed magic."

Ling and his friends exchanged amazed glances, their hearts swelling with gratitude. They had embarked on this journey hoping to make a difference, and now, nature itself was rewarding their bravery and love for the forest.

The deer inclined its head gracefully and continued, "But your work is not yet complete, for there are still those who seek to harm this precious land. You must gather others who share your passion and inspire them to protect and cherish nature."

Ling nodded solemnly, fully understanding the weight of their responsibility. The enchanted glade had bestowed upon them not only its beauty but also a mission to spread awareness and rally more defenders of the forest.

With renewed determination, Ling and his companions ventured forth, sharing stories of their journey, planting saplings, and encouraging others to join their cause. The once desolate forest blossomed with life, as animals returned to their homes and the songs of birds filled the air.

As Ling and his friends continued their mission, they were heartened to see more people joining their cause. Word spread like wildfire, and the once-threatened forest became a symbol of hope and resilience.

Gazing at the vibrant colors and listening to nature's melodies, Ling felt a sense of profound fulfillment. His wise monkey heart swelled with pride, knowing that their actions had made a tangible difference in the world.

But Ling also knew that their journey was not over yet. There were still more people to inspire, more forests to protect, and more stories to tell. Ling looked at Mei, Sora, and the children, and they all shared a silent understanding and a commitment to never stop fighting for the beauty and harmony of nature.

As they ventured further into the enchanted glade, Ling couldn't help but wonder what other wonders and challenges awaited them. With anticipation and unwavering determination, they set off on their next adventure, eager to make an even greater impact on the world they held so dear.

## Chapter 26

As the days turned into weeks, Ling and his friends noticed a change in the forest. The air felt heavy, and a sense of unease lingered in the atmosphere. The once vibrant meadow had lost its luster, the flowers drooping and the stream running dry. Ling's heart sank as he saw the signs of something sinister happening.

The animals whispered amongst themselves, their voices filled with worry. Ling gathered his friends and the children, their faces etched with concern. They knew they couldn't let the forest slip into darkness again.

Together, they ventured deeper into the forest, following the trail of destruction. The trees stood tall, but their leaves were withering, their branches brittle and lifeless. Ling's heart ached at the sight, but he refused to lose hope.

They soon stumbled upon a small village that had sprung up at the edge of the forest. Smoke billowed from chimneys, and the sound of axes striking wood echoed through the air.

Their eyes widened with horror as they realized the villagers were cutting down the trees, fueled by greed and ignorance. Ling's determination deepened, and he knew they had to stop them before it was too late.

Gathering his friends and the children together, Ling devised a plan. They would confront the villagers and try to make them understand the importance of the forest. Armed with courage and conviction, they set off toward the village.

They arrived just as the final tree fell, the deafening sound tearing through the silence of the forest. Ling's heart shattered, but he knew they had to try.

They approached the village with caution, but the villagers greeted them with hostility. Ling's voice trembled as he spoke, urging them to see the beauty and value of the forest. But his words fell on deaf ears.

The villagers scoffed, dismissing Ling's pleas as foolishness. They saw the forest as nothing more than a means to their ends a source of wealth and progress.

Determined not to give up, Ling and his friends turned to leave, but their path was blocked by the villagers. Anger filled the villagers' eyes as they shouted insults and threats, forcing Ling and his friends into a corner.

Fear gripped the children, but Ling's voice rang out, filled with strength and conviction. He reminded them of the bond between humans and nature, and how their actions would have lasting consequences.

Slowly, the villagers began to listen. Ling's words touched something deep within their hearts, reminding them of the beauty they were about to destroy. Regret crept into their eyes as they realized the gravity of their actions.

Tears streamed down Ling's face as he watched the villagers drop their weapons and step back. They had made a connection, bridging the gap between humans and nature.

But Ling knew their mission was far from over. The forest still needed their protection, and they would continue their fight to heal the land and inspire others to do the same.

With renewed determination, Ling led his friends and the children back into the heart of the forest. As they walked, the sun began to peek through the clouds, casting a warm glow upon their path.

The story had turned darker, but Ling held onto the hope of brighter days ahead. He knew that together, they could bring back the light and save their beloved sanctuary. The forest needed them now more than ever, and Ling was ready to face the challenges that lay ahead.

## Chapter 27

As the days turned into weeks, Ling and his friends noticed a stark change in the forest they had worked so hard to protect. The once-vibrant meadow had lost its luster, the sparkling stream had turned murky, and the trees stood withered and frail.

Ling's heart sank as he witnessed the devastating aftermath of human greed. The villagers, who had momentarily dropped their weapons when confronted, had now resumed their destructive ways. They continued to cut down the trees with reckless abandon, oblivious to the irreversible damage they were causing.

Ling, Mei, Sora, and the children stood in disbelief, their eyes filled with tears as they saw the once-thriving ecosystem crumble before them. Ling's voice trembled as he tried to reason with the villagers once more, pleading for them to understand the consequences of their actions.

But this time, his pleas fell on deaf ears. The villagers had grown callous and hardened, blinded by their selfish desires. They scoffed at Ling's words, dismissing him as nothing more than a mere monkey.

Undeterred by their ignorance, Ling turned to his friends for support. Mei's eyes blazed with determination, and Sora's wings fluttered with resolve. They knew they couldn't give up now, not when their mission was more crucial than ever.

Together, they devised a plan to confront the villagers, not with words, but with a visual reminder of what they were destroying. Ling and his friends gathered the fallen leaves, withered branches, and dried flowers from the dying forest.

They carefully arranged them in the shape of a majestic tree, creating a monument that embodied the beauty and life that had once thrived in their sanctuary. Ling hoped that this visual representation would ignite a spark of empathy in the villagers' hearts, reminding them of what they were losing.

As dawn broke, Ling and his friends placed the monument in the heart of the desolate meadow, right where the villagers would pass on their way to continue their destructive mission. They stepped back, their hearts heavy but hopeful, as they awaited the villagers' arrival.

When the villagers finally approached, their eyes fell upon the monument. At first, their expressions remained unchanged, their hearts still hardened by greed. But as they took a closer look, their faces shifted, their features contorted by a mix of guilt and realization.

Ling watched as tears welled up in the eyes of some villagers, their hands trembling as they reached out to touch the delicate branches and faded leaves. Ling's voice broke through the silence, his words laden with sorrow yet filled with an unwavering resolve.

"Our home is dying, and we are all responsible. But it's not too late to make amends," Ling's voice echoed through the meadow. "We can still choose to save what remains of our sanctuary, protect the forest and the creatures that call it home."

As Ling's words hung in the air, a

transformation began in the villagers. One by one, they dropped their axes and saws, embracing the weight of their actions. Ling's determination had pierced through their hearts, awakening their dormant sense of responsibility towards nature.

United by a shared purpose, Ling, Mei, Sora, and the villagers vowed to restore the forest to its former glory. With renewed determination, they set out to replant the trees, nurture the soil, and revive the once-vibrant ecosystem.

The road ahead was still fraught with challenges, but Ling and his friends knew that together, they could make a difference. The journey to protect their beloved sanctuary had taken a darker turn, but their unwavering spirit would guide them toward a brighter future.

And so, Ling and his friends prepared to face the trials that awaited them, ready to fight for the forest and all the creatures that relied on its existence. In the face of adversity, they stood strong, fueled by the belief that even in the darkest of times, light could still be found.

## Chapter 28

In the days that followed, Ling and his friends worked tirelessly to restore the once-thriving forest. They planted new saplings, nourished the soil, and cared for the wounded animals that had lost their homes. It was a daunting task, but their determination never wavered.

The children who had joined Ling's cause proved to be invaluable. They brought forth their youthful energy and eagerness to learn, becoming the forest's greatest advocates. With every passing day, more children from the nearby villages would join them, their faces filled with awe and wonder as they marveled at the beauty of nature.

Ling, Mei, Sora, and the children spent their mornings gathering seeds and their afternoons planting them with great care. They understood that the future of the forest depended on their relentless efforts.

As the forest began to heal, Ling would often find moments of solitude, perched atop his favorite tree branch, deep in thought. He wondered if their mission had truly made a lasting impact. Would the lessons they taught the villagers endure, or would history repeat itself?

His concerns were soon answered when one day, while exploring the outskirts of the forest, Ling and his friends stumbled upon a group of villagers led by the village elder, Elder Song. Their hearts filled with hope as they witnessed the villagers planting trees and building birdhouses with their own hands.

Ling approached Elder Song and asked, "What has changed in your hearts?"

Elder Song sighed, his eyes filled with remorse. "We were blind to the damage we were causing," he said. "But your words and actions opened our eyes. We saw the consequences of our greed, and we realized that it was up to us to make amends."

Ling nodded, a sense of relief washing over him. The villagers had truly understood the importance of their mission, not just for themselves, but for the generations to come.

From that day forward, the villagers worked side by side with Ling and his friends, helping to restore the forest to its former glory. They built bridges and cleared paths, always mindful of the delicate balance between human needs and the well-being of nature.

Word of their efforts spread beyond the villages, reaching the ears of many others who yearned for change. People from far and wide came to witness the miraculous rebirth of the once-threatened forest. Ling's story became a symbol of hope and resilience, inspiring countless others to take action and protect the natural world.

Yet, Ling knew that their mission was far from over. He understood that protecting the forest was an ongoing battle, one that required continuous love, dedication, and education. With each passing day, Ling saw the forest and its inhabitants thrive, and he was grateful for the opportunity to be their guardian.

As Ling looked out at the thriving forest, he knew that he and his friends had made a difference. The wise monkey smiled, his heart filled with joy and gratitude, as he prepared for the next chapter of their journey to protect and cherish nature, one step at a time.

## Chapter 29

Days turned into weeks, and the forest began to flourish once again. The once-barren meadow was now a vibrant tapestry of wildflowers, their colors dancing in the gentle breeze. The trees stood tall and strong, their leaves rustling with a newfound vitality. Ling, Mei, Sora, and the villagers were filled with a sense of accomplishment as they witnessed the fruits of their labor.

Elder Song, his face etched with determination, led the villagers in their restoration efforts. They planted sapling after sapling, ensuring that every inch of the forest would be adorned with the promise of new life. The children, their hearts filled with awe, joined in eagerly, their tiny hands carefully tending to the delicate plants. Ling watched with pride as their dedication mirrored his own.

As the forest bloomed, so did the villagers'

understanding. They began to see the interconnectedness of every living being, realizing that their actions had consequences that reached far beyond themselves. They no longer viewed the forest as merely a resource to exploit, but as a sanctuary to protect, a home to cherish.

Ling continued to share his wisdom with the villagers, reminding them of the delicate balance of nature and the importance of their role as stewards of the land. He taught them how to live harmoniously with the forest, showing them that progress and preservation could coexist. The villagers, once blinded by their greed, now listened intently, their hearts open to the wisdom of the wise monkey.

In the evenings, as the sun dipped below the horizon, Ling and his friends gathered with the villagers around a crackling fire. They shared stories, laughter, and dreams of a future where humans and nature lived in harmony. The children, their eyes shining with hope, spoke of their plans to spread the message beyond the forest, to the farthest corners of the world.

Word of the villagers' transformation spread like wildfire. People from neighboring villages, inspired by their efforts, came to witness the magic of the once-dying forest. Ling, Mei, Sora, and the villagers warmly welcomed them, knowing that their shared experiences would ignite a collective desire to protect nature.

Together, they allied an army of hearts beating in unison with the rhythm of the forest. They vowed to stand against anyone who threatened the delicate balance, armed not with weapons, but with knowledge, compassion, and a fierce determination to protect the precious gift of life.

As the moon smiled down upon the forest, Ling knew that their work was far from complete. There were still battles to be fought, minds to be changed, and lessons to be learned. But with each passing day, Ling and his friends saw the transformation in the villagers' hearts, the once-gray world around them blooming with vibrant colors.

The wise monkey knew that the journey had only just begun. Together, they would continue to protect the forest, nurturing its beauty and guarding its secrets. They would inspire others to make a difference, to see the world through compassionate eyes, and to understand that every choice mattered.

And so, Ling, Mei, Sora, and the villagers stood united in their mission, ready to face any challenge that came their way. With hope as their guide, they would ensure that the wise monkey's legacy would live on, written forever in the tapestry of their shared commitment to protect the home they held dear.

## Chapter 30

Ling, Mei, Sora, and the villagers stood side by side, their hearts still brimming with determination. They had witnessed the transformation of the forest, but their work was far from over. The battle was won, but the war against ignorance and destruction continued.

With renewed purpose, Ling and his allies devised a plan to further spread awareness about the importance of conservation. They decided to organize a grand celebration, inviting neighboring villages to witness the restored wonder of the forest.

Elder Song took charge of the arrangements, involving every member of the community. The village square was adorned with hand-painted banners and colorful ribbons, showcasing the vibrant spirit that had been reignited within the villagers' hearts.

On the day of the celebration, the forest

hummed with anticipation. The villagers, dressed in traditional garments, gathered near the entrance of the forest, their eyes shining with excitement. Ling stood tall, overlooking the crowd, ready to address the multitude.

As Ling's wise voice carried through the air, the villagers listened intently. He spoke of their journey, the harsh consequences of their past actions, and the transformative power of unity and compassion. Ling's words inspired hope and ignited a fire within each villager's soul, as they realized the impact they could make together.

With fervor in their hearts, the villagers formed small groups, each assigned a specific task to contribute to the ongoing conservation efforts. Some were responsible for documenting the growth of the forest, capturing its beauty through paintings and photographs. Others took charge of educating nearby villages about the importance of preservation.

Ling and his allies continued to nurture the forest, planting more saplings and monitoring the well-being of the animals. They knew that the support of the villagers provided a solid foundation for a sustainable future.

Months passed, and the once-depleted forest transformed into a lush paradise. The trees grew tall and strong, their leaves radiating with vibrant green hues. The sounds of animals echoed through the woods, a testament to the vibrant ecosystem that had been restored.

The celebration became an annual tradition, a gathering of communities from far and wide, all united by their shared love for nature. Together, they marveled at the forest's recovery, vowing to safeguard it for generations to come.

Ling and his allies remained at the heart of the village, their wisdom and guidance continuing to inspire all who encountered them. They knew that the battle against human greed was ongoing, but with the collective efforts of the villagers and the lessons learned, their cause would endure.

As the sun dipped below the horizon, casting a warm glow over the forest, Ling, Mei, Sora, and the villagers stood together, their hands linked in a symbol of unity. They knew that their mission was not just about saving a forest; it was about protecting the very essence of life itself.

And so, as the wise monkey and his companions basked in the support and love of their newfound allies, they remained steadfast in their commitment to preserving nature's delicate balance. For they understood that the power of unity and the resilience of the human spirit could conquer any challenge, ensuring a brighter and greener future for all.

## Chapter 31

Time passed, and the forest thrived under the watchful eyes of Ling, Mei, Sora, and the villagers. The once barren areas were now adorned with lush greenery, and the animals rejoiced as their habitats flourished once again. The bond between humans and nature grew stronger each day.

In the heart of the village, Elder Song had called a meeting. Ling, Mei, Sora, and the children gathered around, eager to hear what the elder had to say. The sun illuminated the clearing, casting a golden glow upon the faces of the villagers.

"Ling, my wise friend," Elder Song began, his voice filled with gratitude, "we owe you and your friends an immeasurable debt of gratitude. Through your courage and wisdom, you have given us hope and shown us the power of unity. The forest has been restored, but our work is far from over."

All eyes turned to Ling, awaiting his response. The wise monkey smiled, his eyes glimmering with determination. "Elder Song, my journey began with a mission to protect this forest. Now, it has become so much more. Together, we have not only restored the land but also transformed the hearts of the villagers. We have shown them the true value of nature, and I believe in their ability to carry this mission forward."

The children, inspired by Ling's words, exchanged excited whispers. Mei, with an encouraging nod, stepped forward. "We have seen the change within this community, but there are still many more lives to touch. Ling and I have traveled far and wide, encountering other forests in need. We must extend our reach beyond this village and share our knowledge with others."

The villagers exchanged uncertain glances, unsure of what Mei proposed. Ling, sensing their hesitancy, stepped forward. "I understand your concern, but the world is vast, and our duty to protect it extends far beyond our home. By spreading our message, we can bring about lasting change for all forests threatened by human greed."

A newfound sense of purpose ignited within the villagers. They realized that their journey had just begun, and their commitment to protect nature transcended their own village's borders.

Elder Song raised his hand, signaling for the gathering's attention. "Ling, Mei, Sora, and the children, I speak for all of us when I say that we are with you. Our village will continue to safeguard this forest, but we will also support your journey to protect other lands and inspire more communities. Our alliance reaches beyond our borders."

The air buzzed with excitement as Ling and his friends felt the weight of responsibility, but also the strength of the villagers' support. Together, they would embark on a new chapter, determined to spread the message of conservation and protect nature wherever it faced threat.

Under the shade of the ancient oak tree, Ling knew that their mission would be challenging, but the villagers' newfound passion and the bond they shared would give them the strength they needed. The wise monkey's heart swelled with gratitude for the opportunity to lead this remarkable alliance.

And so, Ling's call echoed through the village, spreading into the depths of the forest and reaching the farthest corners of the land. It was a call for unity, courage, and the protection of the natural world. Ling and his friends stood tall, ready to answer that call, knowing that together they would make a difference, one forest at a time.

## Chapter 32

As the days grew shorter and the nights grew longer, a shadow loomed over the once-thriving forest. Ling, Mei, Sora, and the villagers had worked tirelessly to restore the land, but a new threat emerged, casting a dark cloud upon their hopes.

Whispers of greed and destruction drifted through the village, and rumors of a group of loggers planning to cut down the neighboring forest reached Ling's ears. Fear gnawed at his heart, knowing that if they succeeded, all their hard work would be in vain.

Ling called an emergency meeting in the village square, the glow of torches illuminating concerned faces. He stood before the crowd, his wise eyes filled with determination.

"We have come so far," Ling began, his voice steady but laced with worry. "But now, our forest faces a new danger. We cannot allow the loggers to destroy what we have fought so hard to restore."

Elder Song stepped forward, his aged face etched with lines of worry and resolve. "Ling is right," he declared. "Our mission to protect the forest must continue. We cannot let greed triumph over nature."

The villagers, though anxious, rallied behind Ling and Elder Song, determined to fight for their newfound paradise. Together, they devised a plan to confront the loggers, using peaceful means of protest and education to persuade them to reconsider their actions.

Day after day, Ling and his companions stood at the forest's edge, holding signs and speaking passionately about the importance of preserving nature. They engaged in conversations with the loggers, sharing stories of the forest's wonder and the creatures that called it home.

However, their efforts seemed to fall on deaf ears. The loggers scoffed at their pleas, driven solely by their desire for profit. Ling's heart sank, feeling the weight of disillusionment settles upon his shoulders. The once-hopeful villagers grew weary, their spirits dampened by the loggers' relentless pursuit.

But Ling refused to give up.

He retreated to the sacred grove, seeking solace amidst the ancient trees. Meditating in silence, he allowed the wisdom of the forest to flow through him. It whispered words of resilience, reminding him of the strength that lay within.

Armed with newfound determination, Ling emerged from the grove with a plan. He gathered the villagers once more, their eyes searching his face for a glimmer of hope. Ling spoke of unity, of finding allies beyond their village to join their cause.

"We cannot fight this battle alone," Ling declared. "We need to reach out to those who understand the true value of nature. It is time to seek allies beyond these woods."

The villagers, though skeptical, trusted Ling's wisdom. Together, they set out on a journey, venturing beyond their familiar forest into unknown territories. They sought out like-minded communities, sharing their stories and struggles, hoping to ignite a flame of resistance against the darkness encroaching upon the world.

As they traveled, Ling's heart ached, knowing that their path ahead would be filled with challenges and uncertainty. But he clung to the hope that in their darkest hour, a spark of light would emerge, illuminating the path towards a future where nature and humanity could coexist in harmony.

And so, with determination in their hearts, Ling, Mei, Sora, and the villagers embarked on a perilous journey, ready to face whatever lay ahead. Little did they know that their quest would take them to the edge of despair before they could reclaim the light of hope.

## Chapter 33

Ling's heart sunk as they ventured deeper into the heart of the forest. There was an unease in the air, a foreboding presence that whispered tales of destruction and despair. The once vibrant colors now seemed muted, as if the forest itself mourned the looming threat.

News of the loggers' relentless pursuit of profit had spread like wildfire, and Ling and the villagers knew they had to act swiftly. They journeyed through dense undergrowth, their footsteps muffled by fallen leaves, fear etched on their faces.

With each passing day, Ling's wise eyes grew heavier, burdened by the weight of the fight ahead. His fur bristled with determination, but also with a sense of urgency. Time was slipping through their fingers, and the forest's fate hung in the balance.

As they emerged from a thicket into a small

clearing, Mei gasped. Before they stood a group of creatures, their eyes glossy with malevolence. Ling recognized them as the trickster spirits, known for their ability to manipulate, scoffing at the delicate harmony that had been restored.

The trickster spirits had aligned themselves with the loggers, enticed by the promise of chaos. Ling knew they had to confront this new threat head-on, for the resistance they needed to build was threatened from within.

But the trickster spirits were cunning, weaving their webs of deception. They whispered lies into the ears of the villagers, sowing seeds of doubt and confusion. Ling watched as trust crumbled, replaced by fear and suspicion.

With unwavering determination, Ling confronted the trickster spirits, his voice strong and steady. He reminded them of the peace they had fought for, the balance they had strived to uphold. But his words fell on deaf ears, as the trickster spirits reveled in chaos, relishing in the turmoil they had invoked.

Darkness spread like ink across the forest, engulfing the once hopeful hearts of the villagers. Ling watched as cracks formed within their unity, their resolve waning under the weight of fear.

Still, Ling refused to give up. He gathered Mei, Sora, and the remaining villagers, their eyes shining with flickering hope. Together, they devised a plan to expose the trickster's spirits and rekindle the flame of unity.

They organized a grand spectacle, a dance of shadows, to unveil the trickster spirits' true intentions. Ling, Mei, Sora, and the villagers threw themselves into rehearsals, their movements fluid and precise. They channeled their collective strength into a mesmerizing display, hoping to break the trickster spirits' hold on the villagers.

The night of the performance arrived, and whispers of anticipation filled the air. The villagers, once torn apart, are now gathered under a sky heavy with stars, their hearts yearning for the truth.

As the dance unfolded, the trickster spirits' masks of deceit shattered, revealing their true forms. Ling watched as once-entranced eyes widened with realization and anger, the villagers rediscovering the strength that had once bound them together.

In the aftermath, Ling and the villagers stood united, their spirits rekindled, ready to face the onslaught of darkness that awaited them. Armed with renewed purpose, they vowed to protect the forest, come what may.

The path ahead remained treacherous, and the darkness threatened to engulf them all. But Ling knew that as long as they faced it together, their resolve would never falter. In the depths of adversity, he found the strength to carry on, for the forest, for the villagers, and for the future they would fight to protect.

## Chapter 34

The dense forest enveloped Ling and the villagers as they pressed forward, their hearts heavy with concern. Ling knew that the unity they had cherished for so long was now threatened. Whispers of doubt filled the air, tugging at the once unbreakable bond they had forged.

Mei, Sora, and the children walked beside Ling, their eyes reflecting the weight of their shared burden. They had come so far in protecting their beloved sanctuary, but the looming threat of the loggers tested everything they had built.

As they journeyed deeper, the forest became eerily silent, matching the growing tension among the villagers. Ling's wise eyes scanned their surroundings, searching for signs of hope amidst the encroaching darkness. But it seemed as if even the vibrant flora and fauna held their breath, waiting for the villagers to find their strength once more.

Days turned into nights, and still, they pressed on. Ling shared stories of their past successes, reminding the villagers of the miracles they had accomplished through unity and determination. His words became beacons of hope, guiding them through the labyrinth of doubt that threatened to consume them all.

However, not all villagers were convinced by Ling's words. Some began questioning their abilities, and their commitment to the cause. Ling understood their fears but knew that doubt could erode their spirit faster than any external force. He had to find a way to unite them once more, to reignite the fire burning within their souls.

One evening, as the moon illuminated the forest floor, Ling led the weary villagers to a clearing. Amidst the tall trees, a colossal oak stood, its branches reaching toward the sky like fingers yearning for connection. Ling gestured for everyone to gather around the ancient tree, its bark weathered and wise.

"This tree," Ling began, his voice firm yet gentle, "is a symbol of unity. Its roots intertwine, supporting one another, just as we must support each other."

He paused, allowing the words to sink in, before continuing, "Each one of you is a branch on this tree, connected to the whole. Alone, you may sway in the wind, but together, you can weather any storm."

Ling urged the villagers to close their eyes and place their hands on the tree's sturdy trunk. He guided them through a meditation, encouraging them to feel the energy that flowed through the ancient oak, connecting them all.

As they stood there, their hands pressed against the rough bark, a warmth began to spread from their fingertips, intertwining like the roots of the tree. Slowly, the doubts that had plagued them melted away, replaced by a renewed sense of purpose and determination.

When they opened their eyes, tears glistened, reflecting the moon's glow. Ling smiled, the weight on his heart lifting, as he saw the spark of unity reignite in the villagers' eyes.

"We are stronger together," Ling whispered, his voice carrying on the wind, "and now, we must face the darkness united."

The villagers nodded, and their resolve solidified. Ling's wisdom had once again guided them, reminding them of their shared mission to protect and preserve the forest.

Armed with renewed determination, Ling and the villagers continued their journey, their spirits uplifted by the unity they had rediscovered. The road ahead was treacherous, but with their hearts joined, they were ready to face the challenge head-on.

Little did they know, hidden within the heart of the forest, allies awaited, eager to stand with them against the encroaching darkness. The test of unity had brought them closer, and together, they would ignite a resistance that would challenge the very essence of greed and destruction.

## Chapter 35

As Ling and the villagers ventured deeper into the forest, an unsettling stillness settled upon them. The once vibrant colors had faded, replaced by a murky darkness that seemed to seep into their souls. Ling's wise eyes surveyed the desolation before him, his heart heavy with worry.

Whispers of doubt began to weave their way through the villagers' minds, like insidious tendrils of darkness. Ling could sense their fear, their uncertainty, as the weight of their mission pressed upon their shoulders. He knew that doubts could shatter the unity they had fought so hard to maintain.

One evening, as they gathered around their campfire, Mei spoke up with a voice laced with concern. "Ling, what if we cannot save the forest? What if our efforts are in vain?"

Ling's eyes shimmered with wisdom, his voice

soothing in the flickering light. "Fear is a natural companion on this journey, my dear Mei. But it is in times of darkness that our true strength emerges. Our purpose is to protect, to fight for what is right. We must not let doubt cloud our hearts."

Sora, usually full of determination, hesitated before voicing his concerns. "Ling, what if we are outnumbered? How can we stand against those consumed by greed?"

Ling's eyes gleamed with a resoluteness that silenced their doubts. "Strength is not always measured in numbers, my dear Sora. It resides within our spirits, our unwavering resolve. Remember that our cause is just, and the forest spirits will guide us."

The villagers exchanged glances, their faces etched with both determination and lingering uncertainty. Ling knew that doubts could fester unless addressed, so he led them to a nearby grove, where an ancient tree stood tall and wise.

Gathering around the symbolic tree, the villagers closed their eyes, allowing the ancient spirit of the forest to envelop them. Ling's gentle voice filled the air, imbued with the wisdom of generations past. "Feel the strength of this mighty tree. Its roots run deep, anchoring it against the fiercest storms. Let us find solace in its embrace."

Silence settled upon the grove, broken only by the soft rustle of leaves and the rhythm of their breathing. In this tranquil moment, doubts melted away, replaced by a renewed sense of purpose and unity.

Their spirits rekindled, Ling and the villagers continued deeper into the forest, their hearts filled with determination to protect their beloved sanctuary. Little did they know that shadows lurked just beyond their line of sight, watching their every move.

Unbeknownst to Ling and his allies, a cloaked figure moved through the darkness, whispering words of deceit and manipulation to those desperate enough to listen. Ling's journey had taken a sinister turn, one that would test their resolve and challenge their faith.

As the story took a darker path, Ling and the villagers soon realized that their fight against greed and destruction was not as straightforward as they had hoped. The true nature of their adversaries would soon be revealed, and they would face a choice that would determine the fate of their beloved forest.

## Chapter 36

Ling and the villagers continued their journey through the heart of the forest, their footsteps echoing in the eerie silence. The once vibrant colors had faded, replaced by a somber gray that matched the heaviness in their hearts. Ling pressed forward, determined to find allies to stand against the impending destruction.

As they ventured deeper into the thick foliage, a figure emerged from the shadows. A young woman with emerald-green eyes and flowing auburn hair stood before them, her presence shrouded in mystery. Ling and the villagers exchanged startled glances, unsure of what to make of this unexpected encounter.

"I am Rika," she said, her voice gentle yet filled with an underlying strength. "I have been waiting for you."

Ling stepped forward, his wise eyes studying Rika's face. "Who are you, and why have you been waiting for us?"

Rika smiled knowingly. "I am a guardian of the forest, just like you. I sensed your struggle and knew you would need help."

The villagers shifted uneasily, their skepticism lingering in the air. Mei, ever curious, spoke up. "How can we be sure that you are here to aid us? We have encountered deception before."

Rika's eyes sparkled with understanding. "I understand your concerns, but I assure you, my intentions are pure. I have been observing your journey, and witnessing your determination to protect these sacred lands. I am here to offer my alliance."

Ling's gaze softened, sensing the sincerity in Rika's words. "Tell us, Rika, what skills or knowledge do you bring?"

Rika's smile widened, revealing a glimmer of excitement. "I possess the gift of natural communication. I can listen to the whispers of the trees, the songs of the wind, and the secrets of the animals. Together, we can harness the strength of the forest."

Hope flickered in the villagers' eyes as they contemplated Rika's offer. Ling, ever thoughtful, nodded in approval. "If you truly share our purpose, we welcome you, Rika. Let us unite our skills to protect this land."

As Rika joined their group, Ling could sense a renewed energy among the villagers. The forest seemed to respond to her presence as if acknowledging her as one of its own. They continued their journey, with Rika by their side, each step now filled with a newfound determination.

In the distance, the soft rustling of leaves and the gentle hooting of an owl echoed through the stillness. Ling knew that danger lurked ahead, but with Rika's gift and the unity of the villagers, they were prepared to face whatever awaited them.

Little did they know that their alliance would soon be tested in ways they could never have imagined. Ling, Mei, Sora, and the villagers were about to embark on a journey that would push their courage and loyalty to their very limits.

But for now, they embraced the presence of the mysterious wanderer, grateful for the strength and hope she brought to their cause. Ling looked ahead, his eyes filled with determination, ready to face the challenges that lay in their path and protect their beloved sanctuary, together.

## Chapter 37

As Ling and the villagers continued their journey through the dense forest, a soft rustle caught their attention. They turned their heads to find a young girl emerging from behind a large oak tree. She had vibrant blue eyes that sparkled with curiosity, and her long, flowing hair was the color of autumn leaves.

"I'm Luna," she said, her voice gentle and soothing. "I've been watching you from afar, and I couldn't help but be drawn to your mission to protect the forest."

Ling studied Luna, his wise eyes seeing something special in her. "We welcome your presence, Luna," he said warmly. "Tell us, why have you come?"

A small smile played on Luna's lips as she stepped closer. "I possess a unique gift," she explained. "I can communicate with the plants and animals in the forest. They shared with me tales of your bravery and unwavering determination."

The villagers exchanged glances, their astonishment evident. Mei stepped forward, her voice filled with hope. "Luna, can this gift of yours truly help us in our fight against those who wish to harm our home?"

Luna nodded, her blue eyes shining with conviction. "The forest is my sanctuary, just as it is yours," she said. "I have heard their cries for help and felt their despair. Together, we can restore harmony and protect this sacred land."

Ling, his heart filled with gratitude, extended his hand toward Luna. "Welcome, Luna. Your gift is a precious addition to our cause."

With a sense of newfound purpose, the group continued their journey, Luna by their side. She guided them through hidden trails and introduced them to mystical creatures that dwelled deep within the forest.

As they ventured further, Luna's gift became more evident. Her whispers to the plants brought life and vibrant colors back to the foliage, while her soothing trills harmonized with the songs of the birds, strengthening their spirits.

With each step, their unity grew stronger, their doubts fading away like distant echoes. Ling marveled at the power of collective determination and the addition of Luna's gift, knowing that they faced tremendous challenges ahead.

Among the shadows of the forest, Ling and the villagers found solace in Luna's presence. Her gentleness and compassion helped heal their wounds and stoke the fires of hope.

As the sun dipped below the horizon, casting a warm golden glow upon the treetops, Ling and his newfound allies paused to rest. Ling gazed at the canopy above, his eyes filled with gratitude for Luna's arrival and the glimmer of hope she brought.

Little did they know, their journey was far from over. The darkest hour loomed, testing their courage and loyalty. But with their unity and the power of Luna's gift, they would face the upcoming challenges head-on, ready to protect their beloved forest.

Together, Ling, Luna, Mei, Sora, and the villagers stood, their hearts intertwining like the branches of a mighty tree. They were ready to face whatever lay ahead, for they knew that their bond was unbreakable.

The wise monkey and his companions prepared to rise with the dawn, their spirits filled with determination. They would not rest until every corner of the forest was reclaimed, and the balance between humans and nature was restored.

And so, with the moon guiding their way, they embarked on the next leg of their journey, eager to confront the darkness and emerge triumphant in their quest to safeguard their sanctuary.

## Chapter 38

Ling and the villagers journeyed deeper into the heart of the forest, their footsteps echoing through the dense undergrowth. As they walked, an unsettling stillness washed over them, causing their hearts to race with concern.

"The forest feels different," Sora whispered, her voice filled with unease. "It's as if the very spirit of these woods has been shaken."

Ling nodded, his wise eyes scanning their surroundings. "Something is not right. We must remain vigilant."

The colors of the foliage seemed muted, the vibrant greens fading into a dull gray. Ling led the way, guiding his companions toward a grove he knew would provide solace and renewed purpose.

With heavy hearts, Ling and the villagers entered the grove, hoping for a respite from the growing tension. They found themselves surrounded by gnarled trees and delicate wildflowers, their petals drooping with a hint of sadness.

Mei reached out and touched a withering blossom. "Oh, Ling, how can we restore harmony to this forest when even the flowers seem to mourn?"

Ling placed a comforting hand on Mei's shoulder. "We may not have all the answers yet, but we must remain steadfast in our mission. Together, we can bring back the vibrancy this forest once knew."

But as they gathered their thoughts and prepared to continue their journey, a powerfully built figure emerged from the shadows. It was Rika, the enigmatic woman they had encountered earlier, her eyes gleaming with an intensity that made the villagers step back.

"Rika," Ling said cautiously, "what brings you here? Have you sensed the disturbance that plagues this forest?"

Rika smiled, but there was a hint of darkness in her expression. "Oh, Ling, you and your villagers are noble in your cause. But even the noblest of hearts can be misled."

Confusion clouded Ling's face. "What do you mean, Rika? We seek only to protect and restore the balance of this land."

Rika's voice dropped to a whisper, and her words carried a chilling warning. "Beware, for there is a hidden trap waiting for you. The very essence of this forest has been tainted by a power far greater than you can fathom."

Ling's eyes narrowed. "Who would dare harm this sanctuary?"

Rika's gaze hardened, and she pointed toward a distant mountain range. "High above, the greedy ones have found a way to harness the forest's energy, siphoning it for their gain. They will stop at nothing to exploit its power."

The villagers gasped in disbelief, their hearts heavy with a newfound understanding of the gravity of their quest.

Ling, determined to face this sinister turn, turned to his companions. "My friends, we have underestimated the forces we face. But fear not, for we have each other, and the strength of our convictions. We will face this challenge head-on."

With renewed determination, Ling and the villagers prepared to confront the hidden trap that awaited them. They would need all their courage and loyalty to protect their beloved sanctuary and restore the balance that had been shattered.

As they ventured forth, unaware of the darkness lurking ahead, Ling whispered a silent prayer for the resilience of the forest and the unity of their cause. The journey ahead would test their resolve, but their hearts burned with the flame of hope, ready to face whatever challenges came their way.

## Chapter 39

Ling and the villagers stood at the edge of the grove, their eyes fixed on Rika's solemn expression. Her words lingered in the air, sending waves of uncertainty rippling through their hearts. Ling's grip on his staff tightened as he scanned their surroundings, his sharp eyes searching for any hidden danger.

"What do you mean by the exploitation of the forest's power?" Ling asked, breaking the tense silence.

Rika sighed, her gaze shifting towards the shadows dancing among the trees. "There is a darkness that lurks deep within this forest a force that seeks to harness its magic for their sinister purposes. They will stop at nothing to control its ancient energy," she explained, her voice heavy with concern.

Luna, with her hands softly caressing a nearby plant, spoke up. "But why would anyone want to harm such a beautiful place? The forest is meant to be protected, cherished," she said, her voice full of innocence.

Rika's eyes softened as she turned to Luna. "Not everyone understands or values the harmony of nature, young one. Some believe that power and control lie in dominance, not unity."

A shiver ran down Mei's spine as the wind carried a faint whisper that seemed to call out to her. "What can we do to stop them, Rika?"

Rika's gaze met each of theirs, her determination shining brightly. "We must uncover the truth and find those responsible. But be warned, dear friends, the path ahead is treacherous, filled with peril and uncertainty."

Sora stepped forward, her voice resolute. "We have come too far to turn back now. Ling, you taught us to fight for what we believe in. We cannot let the forest be consumed by darkness. We must protect it with all we have."

Ling nodded, feeling the weight of responsibility settle on his shoulders. He knew that their journey would only grow more challenging, but he also believed in the resilience and power of unity. "We shall face this darkness head-on. Together, we will overcome any obstacle," he declared, his voice determined.

As the group moved deeper into the forest, the air grew heavy, and the once vibrant colors faded even more. The path became narrower and more treacherous, their steps cautious but unwavering. Ling and his companions were prepared to face whatever awaited them, their hearts intertwined with the spirit of the forest.

Unknown to them, hidden within the shadows, a pair of eyes watched their every move, sinister intentions swirling in their depths. Ling's journey was far from over, and the true extent of the challenge lay just beyond their sight. But with wisdom, courage, and the power of their unity, Ling and the villagers were determined to protect their beloved sanctuary and restore balance to the heart of the forest.

And so, with hope guiding their way, they ventured deeper into the unknown, ready to face the hidden truth that awaited them.

## Chapter 40

Within the depths of the forest, a haunting silence enveloped Ling and the villagers. The atmosphere grew heavier as if the very air held its breath. Shadows danced ominously among the trees, their twisted forms casting eerie shapes upon the forest floor.

As they pressed forward, a deep unease settled in Ling's heart. His senses tingled with an impending danger, urging caution with every step. The once vibrant colors of the foliage now faded, drained of their vitality. Ling's fur stood on end, sensing the dark energy that permeated the grove.

Rika led the way, her piercing gaze scanning the surroundings. Her voice quivered with apprehension as she shared the grim truth that awaited them. "Beware," she warned, "for within this forest, an ancient power has awakened. It seeks to consume everything in its path."

The villagers exchanged worried glances, their expressions mirroring Ling's growing concern. Their determination wavered as the true gravity of their mission became clear. Ling tightened his grip on the staff that lay beside him, drawing strength from its presence.

They journeyed deeper into the heart of darkness, the very essence of the forest twisting around them like a suffocating vine. Strange whispers echoed through the trees, their words too faint to comprehend, yet carrying an unsettling weight.

Every step forward felt like a battle against an invisible force, attempting to push them back, to deter them from their purpose. Ling closed his eyes, summoning the wisdom of his ancestors, drawing upon their knowledge and strength.

Soon, they entered a clearing where a towering tree stood, its branches gnarled and twisted like the grasping hands of the forest itself. At its base, a swirling black mass churned with malevolent energy. Ling's heart sank as he recognized the source of the darkness.

Before them, a creature emerged, its form shifting and contorting with a sickening fluidity. Its eyes glowed with a maleficent light, and a chilling voice echoed through the clearing. "You dare to challenge me, mortals? The forest is mine to command!"

Ling's voice trembled, but he refused to yield. "We stand united, to protect the balance of nature. You will not consume this forest!"

With a sinister laugh, the creature lunged forward, its darkness stretching toward Ling and the villagers. Their weapons clashed against the encroaching shadows, determination fueling their every strike.

But the darkness proved relentless, growing stronger with each passing moment. Ling felt his strength wane, his spirit threatened to be consumed. The weight of doubt pressed heavily upon him as if the very essence of the forest was against them.

In the face of this unyielding darkness, Ling knew that their resolve had to shine brighter. It was in this darkness that their true strength would emerge. With a surge of courage, Ling rallied his comrades, their spirits intertwining in a web of unwavering determination.

Together, they fought against the consuming darkness, refusing to let the forest be lost to its grasp. Their voices rose above the chaos, echoing a chorus of unity and defiance.

And as the battle raged on, a glimmer of hope flickered within Ling's heart. For he knew that no matter how dark the path, the light of their unwavering commitment to protect the forest would guide their way.

## Chapter 41

Ling and the villagers emerged from the darkness, their hearts pounding with adrenaline and hope. The air felt lighter as if the weight of their fears had been lifted.

As they walked further into the forest, they noticed a soft glow emanating from the trees above. Curiosity piqued, Ling motioned for everyone to follow him. They came upon a clearing, where rays of sunlight streamed through the leaves, creating a magical dance of light and shadow.

In the center of the clearing, they found a circle of flowers, each one radiating a different hue. It was a breathtaking sight. Ling and the villagers couldn't help but smile, captivated by the beauty that surrounded them.

Suddenly, a gentle breeze rustled the leaves and a voice whispered in the wind. "Welcome, protectors of the forest," it spoke. Startled yet intrigued, Ling turned toward the sound.

There, sitting on a bed of moss, was an ethereal being a pixie with shimmering wings that resembled delicate petals. Her eyes sparkled with wisdom and kindness. Ling couldn't help but feel a sense of familiarity in her presence.

"Ling, Mei, Sora, and the children," the pixie said, her voice melodic. "You have shown great courage and determination. The forest is grateful for your unwavering dedication."

Ling's heart swelled with pride, knowing that their efforts were making a difference. "We are honored," he replied, his voice filled with gratitude.

The pixie smiled warmly. "There is still much to be done, but fear not, for you are not alone. The forest has chosen you as its champions, and it will guide you on your journey."

With those words, the pixie gracefully rose from her mossy perch and floated closer to Ling and the villagers. She gently touched each of their foreheads, transferring a soft glow that filled their beings with renewed energy.

"As long as you walk alongside nature, you will be granted its blessings," the pixie whispered.

"Remember, the power of the forest lies within you."

Ling and the villagers felt a surge of warmth as if the forest's vitality had become a part of them. They exchanged glances, their hearts filled with determination and a newfound sense of purpose.

With a final wave of her hand, the pixie vanished, leaving Ling and the villagers in awe of the magical encounter they had just experienced. They knew that this encounter marked a turning point in their journey, a beacon of hope that would guide them forward.

Renewed and filled with a renewed sense of purpose, Ling and the villagers continued their mission to protect and restore the forest. Armed with the forest's blessings and their unwavering commitment, they moved forward with a lightness in their steps, ready to face whatever challenges lay ahead.

Little did they know that their encounter with the pixie was just the beginning of an extraordinary adventure that would test their resilience, their bonds, and ultimately, the strength of their connection to the heart of the forest.

## Chapter 42

Ling and the villagers stood in awe, their eyes widened with wonder as they took in the sight before them. The magical clearing was bathed in a soft, golden light, casting a warm glow on the lush vegetation that surrounded them. The air carried a sweet, intoxicating scent as if the very essence of the forest was infused with enchantment.

In the center of the clearing stood a magnificent tree, its branches stretching towards the heavens, reaching for the stars. Its leaves shimmered in a myriad of colors, reflecting the hopes and dreams of all who had come before. Ling felt a surge of gratitude well up inside him, knowing that they were chosen to stand in this sacred place.

The ethereal pixie, her delicate wings fluttering, floated forward, her voice as gentle as a breeze. "Welcome, brave protectors of the forest," she whispered, her words carrying a sense of ancient wisdom. "You have faced the darkness and emerged victorious, proving yourselves worthy of the forest's guidance."

Ling and the villagers exchanged glances, their hearts filled with a mixture of awe and determination. They understood that their journey was far from over. There was still much they needed to uncover and protect.

"The forest is more than just trees and animals," the pixie continued, her voice resonating with a deep sense of reverence. "It holds the secrets of generations past, the knowledge of balance and harmony, and the power to heal the wounds inflicted upon it. You must safeguard this sacred knowledge."

She reached out her delicate hand, and a glow emanated from her palm. In a shower of shimmering dust, small orbs of light appeared, hovering in the air. The orbs danced playfully, each representing a fragment of the forest's essence.

"These orbs hold the wisdom of ages," the pixie explained. "Each of you shall be entrusted with one. They will serve as your guide and guardian, leading you towards the truth and aiding you in your endeavors."

With a sense of anticipation, Ling and the villagers stepped forward, one by one, extending their hands. The pixie gently placed an orb in each of their palms, the warmth and energy of the forest flowing through their veins.

As the orbs settled into their hands, Ling felt a surge of power and purpose. The forest had chosen them, and they would not disappoint. They were now connected to something greater than themselves, entrusted with the task of unraveling the mysteries hidden within the shadows.

"We must gather the scattered fragments of the forest's power," Ling said, his voice filled with determination. "Only then can we heal the wounds and restore balance."

The villagers nodded in agreement, their eyes shining with determination. Ling knew that the path ahead would be treacherous, but he also knew that they were not alone. With the forest's guidance and their unwavering resolve, they would overcome any obstacle in their way.

Leaving the magical clearing behind, Ling and

the villagers set forth, their hearts filled with the promise of restoration and renewal. The forest whispered its secrets to them, its ancient trees rustling with encouragement.

Together, they would face the challenges that lay ahead, bound by their shared love for the forest and their unwavering determination to protect it. The journey to restore balance had just begun, and Ling and his fellow protectors were ready to be the voice of the forest, to ensure that its wisdom would endure for generations to come.

## Chapter 43

In the radiant glow of the magical clearing, Ling and the villagers marveled at the beauty that surrounded them. They could feel the energy of the forest pulsating through their veins, filling them with an indescribable lightness.

As they took a step forward, the ground beneath their feet seemed to tremble with excitement. Mei's eyes sparkled with joy as she spotted colorful butterflies fluttering amidst the vibrant flowers. Sora couldn't help but laugh, his laughter echoing through the clearing like a sweet melody.

Ling grinned, his wise eyes gleaming with pride. This was the moment they had been working towards, the culmination of their efforts to protect and restore the forest. The weight of their previous battles seemed to lift off their shoulders, replaced by a renewed sense of hope and determination.

Together, they began their journey through the forest, guided by the whispers of the wind and the gentle sway of the trees. Each step felt lighter than the last as if the forest itself were lifting them, urging them forward.

Along their path, they encountered various creatures who greeted them with curiosity and kindness. Ling watched with a twinkle in his eye as the children exchanged playful banter with a family of mischievous squirrels, their laughter echoing through the forest.

As they ventured deeper, the villagers noticed the positive changes that had started taking place. The once barren patches of land were now filled with saplings, their tender green leaves reaching for the sun. The air was cleaner, the songs of birds resonating through the canopy once more.

But amidst the newfound beauty, Ling couldn't help but sense a lingering darkness. It was faint, like a distant memory, but he knew that their task was far from over. There were still secrets to uncover and challenges to overcome.

Gathering the villagers around him, Ling spoke

with unwavering determination. "We have come so far, my friends, and we have witnessed the incredible healing power of this forest. But we must remain vigilant. The darkness that once threatened our home may linger in the shadows, waiting for a chance to return. We must continue to protect and restore, to ensure that this forest thrives for generations to come."

The villagers nodded, their eyes filled with determination. Though the journey ahead was uncertain, their hearts were brimming with hope. Ling's wise words had anchored their spirits, reminding them of the importance of their mission.

As they continued their exploration, their laughter filled the forest once more. Ling knew that they were not just saving the physical aspect of the forest but also its soul. With each step they took, the forest responded, embracing them with its eternal gratitude.

The story of Ling and the villagers would resonate far beyond their forest. Their journey would inspire others to take a stand, to protect the natural wonders that surrounded them. Ling's wisdom would be remembered, his legacy forever etched into the hearts of those who dared to dream and make a difference.

With the forest as their guide, Ling and the villagers stepped into the unknown, ready to face whatever challenges lay ahead. Their spirits were light, their resolve unbreakable. For as long as they stood together, nothing could extinguish the flame of hope that burned within their hearts.

## Chapter 44

As Ling and the villagers continued their journey to protect and restore the forest, they stumbled upon a narrow path shrouded in mist. Intrigued, they cautiously followed the winding trail, their footsteps barely making a sound.

Suddenly, a gentle rustling of leaves drew their attention. Ling signaled for the others to halt, and they peered through the foliage. There, standing amidst the swirling mist, was a figure they had never seen before.

The stranger had long silver hair that cascaded down their back, shimmering like moonlight. Their eyes held a mysterious gleam, filled with ancient wisdom. Dressed in flowing robes adorned with intricate patterns, the newcomer exuded an aura of tranquility.

"Who are you?" Ling called out, his voice filled with curiosity.

The stranger turned towards them, a serene smile playing on their lips. "I am known as Kaida," they replied, their voice soft yet commanding. "I am a wanderer, a guardian of forgotten places, and a seeker of hidden knowledge."

Mei stepped forward, her eyes gleaming with excitement. "Are you here to help us protect the forest, Kaida?"

Kaida nodded, their gaze filled with purpose. "Indeed, young ones. I have sensed the powerful connection you all share with this sacred place. The forest has chosen you for a reason, and I am here to guide you on your path."

Sora stepped forward, her movements fluid and graceful. "What can you teach us, Kaida? We have encountered many challenges on our journey. We seek to understand the lingering darkness that threatens the forest."

Kaida's eyes sparkled with understanding. "To overcome the darkness, you must first seek the light within yourselves. The forest's wisdom flows through each of you, waiting to be awakened."

The children's eyes widened with anticipation, and Ling glanced at his fellow villagers, a newfound sense of hope coursing through their veins. Kaida's arrival had breathed new life into their mission.

As they continued their journey, Kaida shared stories of ancient rituals and the importance of harmony between humans and nature. They also revealed hidden secrets of the forest, guiding Ling and the villagers deeper into its heart.

At nightfall, they gathered around a crackling fire, sharing tales of their adventures. Kaida emphasized the importance of unity and resilience, reminding them that their combined strength would be the key to success.

With each passing day, Ling and the villagers felt their bond deepen, their hearts entwined with the forest's rhythm. Kaida's guidance and wisdom fueled their determination to protect and restore the sacred land, renewing their purpose.

Little did they know, further challenges awaited them on their path. But with Kaida by their side, Ling and his village felt a renewed sense of courage and an unyielding desire to preserve the wisdom of the forest.

Together, they would face whatever darkness lay ahead, for they were the chosen guardians, entrusted with the sacred task of ensuring the forest's legacy thrived for generations to come.

# Chapter 45

Ling and the villagers followed Kaida as she led them further into the heart of the enchanted forest. The air grew thicker, and the sound of rustling leaves filled their ears. The path they traversed was narrow, covered in a vibrant carpet of moss that seemed to glow under the dappling sunlight.

As they pressed on, Mei spotted a curious sight. "Look!" she whispered, pointing to a small creature with shimmering wings flitting among the tall ferns. "It's a forest sprite!"

The sprite, a tiny creature with luminous blue skin and twinkling eyes, paused in mid-air, observing the group through a mischievous smile. Ling recognized the sprite as one of the forest's guardians.

"Hello, little one," Ling greeted softly. "We mean no harm. We are here to protect and restore the wisdom of the forest."

The sprite's wings fluttered, and it hovered closer, its tiny voice filling the air. "You have proven your intentions are pure," it chimed. "Follow the hidden path to unravel the secrets that lie within."

With a mischievous giggle, the sprite darted away, disappearing into the foliage. Ling and the villagers exchange glances filled with anticipation. The hidden path, the next step on their journey, beckoned them.

Through the dense undergrowth, the group followed Kaida's lead, their every step filled with purpose. They maneuvered around gnarled roots and ducked beneath low-hanging branches, their determination never wavering.

As they forged ahead, Ling noticed a soft humming sound growing louder and more distinct. The closer they approached, the more apparent it became a hidden waterfall, cascading down a rocky cliff, shimmering in the sunlight.

Gazing at the mesmerizing sight, the villagers couldn't help but feel awestruck. The water flowed with grace, its crystal-clear droplets sparkling like diamonds. It was as if the forest itself were breathing life into the tranquil oasis.

Kaida motioned them closer, her silver hair glinting in the sunlight. "This waterfall holds a secret," she whispered, her voice almost lost amidst the gentle splashes. "Only those with pure hearts can access the wisdom that lies beyond."

Ling and the villagers exchanged meaningful glances. Each held their intentions pure and true, their love for the forest unwavering. With newfound determination, they approached the waterfall, feeling the gentle spray against their faces.

Taking a collective breath, they stepped through the cascading veil of water and into the hidden chamber behind. As they emerged, their eyes widened at the sight that greeted them.

Before them stood a majestic tree, its branches reaching towards the heavens. Glowing orbs nestled among the leaves, pulsating with radiant energy. Ling and the villagers felt a surge of power as they entered the sacred space, their spirits intertwining with the life force of the forest.

Ling's eyes glimmered with unspoken understanding. They had arrived at the heart of the forest's wisdom, entrusted with the task of gathering the scattered power and restoring harmony. With every breath, they knew their journey had just begun.

Together, Ling, Mei, Sora, the children, and Kaida stood beneath the sacred tree, their hearts filled with hope and purpose. They accepted their role as guardians, knowing that their mission would not only protect the forest but also inspire others to cherish the natural world.

As they immersed themselves in the tranquility of the hidden chamber, they understood that the wisdom they sought was not solely for themselves but to be shared with all who would listen. Ling and the villagers pledged to carry the forest's teachings far beyond its borders, to ignite a spark in the hearts of all who would lend an ear.

United by their shared purpose, Ling and the villagers swore to safeguard the wisdom of the forest, no matter the challenges they may face. Little did they know that their resolve would soon be tested, for darkness still lingered in the shadows, waiting for an opportune moment to strike.

But in this sacred space, surrounded by the forest's benevolent energy, Ling and his companions felt an unyielding strength, ready to face whatever lay ahead. With every beat of their hearts, they embarked on the next stage of their journey, determined to protect the forest and its wisdom at all costs.

## Chapter 46

Ling and the villagers stood in the sacred chamber, feeling the weight of their commitment. The air was thick with anticipation as they prepared to embark on their next task.

Kaida, their newfound companion, approached the center of the chamber, her steps deliberate and graceful. Her silver hair seemed to shimmer in the dim light, and her voice carried a soothing melody as she addressed the group.

"To truly restore harmony in the forest, you must prove your worthiness," Kaida explained, her eyes gleaming with a mixture of wisdom and challenge. "The Guardian's test awaits you."

Ling's heart quickened at the mention of the test. He exchanged glances with Mei, Sora, and the villagers, finding reassurance in their determined expressions. They were ready for whatever awaited them.

Kaida led them to a moss-covered stone door at the back of the chamber. With a gentle touch, the door swung open, revealing a winding path through thick foliage. The air was alive with the scent of blooming flowers and the soft rustle of leaves.

"We must follow this path," Kaida said, her voice filled with certainty. "But be aware, the Guardian will challenge you in ways you cannot yet fathom. Trust in your bond with the forest, and you shall succeed."

Ling took a deep breath, grounding himself in the forest's energy. The group stepped onto the path, their resolve strengthening with each step. The forest around them seemed to come alive, whispering encouragement and offering guidance.

As they ventured deeper into the enchanted forest, their path became treacherous. Thorny obstacles emerged, threatening to hinder their progress. Ling summoned his knowledge of the forest and directed the villagers to maneuver through the prickly maze, their determination unwavering.

Suddenly, a deafening roar echoed through the trees. A magnificent creature, part lion and part eagle emerged from the shadows. Its eyes gleamed with fierce intelligence as it assessed the group.

"The Guardian," Kaida whispered, her voice barely audible above the creature's thunderous presence.

The lion-eagle Guardian loomed over them, testing their mettle. It circled Ling and the villagers, watching their every move. Ling locked eyes with the creature, refusing to show fear. He understood that the Guardian was there to gauge their commitment to protecting the forest.

With a single swift motion, the Guardian lunged at Ling, claws extended. But Ling, quick as lightning, dodged the attack, leaping gracefully to the side. The villagers gasped, their eyes wide with awe.

Ling's instincts kicked in, and he knew the true nature of the Guardian's test. It wasn't physical strength that would prevail but inner strength and the unwavering bond they shared with the forest.

Gathering his courage, Ling closed his eyes and outstretched his hand, connecting with the forest and its vast wisdom. The air shimmered, and a gentle breeze rustled through the leaves, wrapping around Ling protectively.

Witnessing Ling's display of harmony with nature, the Guardian paused, its fierce gaze softening. It lowered its head in acknowledgment and stepped aside, allowing Ling and the villagers to pass.

As they continued their journey, Ling felt a renewed sense of purpose coursing through his veins. The Guardian's test had cemented their commitment, unifying them further. They would face any challenge that came their way, for they were bound by their love and determination to protect the forest.

With each step forward, Ling knew that their mission had only just begun. They had proven themselves to the Guardian, but greater trials awaited them. Ling's grip on Mei's hand tightened, and together they pressed on, ready to face whatever lay ahead in their pursuit of restoring harmony in the forest.

Little did they know, an even greater danger lurked in the shadows, threatening to undo all they had accomplished. But with their unwavering bond and the wisdom of the forest in their hearts, Ling and the villagers were prepared to face it head-on.

## Chapter 47

Ling and the villagers, their hearts filled with newfound determination, followed Kaida deeper into the enchanted forest. The twists and turns of the verdant path revealed hidden wonders at every step. Colors danced with the sunlight, and whispers of ancient magic brushed against their skin.

As they walked, Ling couldn't help but notice the villagers' growing confidence. Their journey had transformed them from ordinary individuals into protectors of nature, and it showed in the way they moved through the forest each step deliberate, each gaze keen with anticipation.

Kaida halted at a clearing, her eyes sparkling with a knowing smile. "Beyond this point lies the heart of the forest," she said, her voice carrying an air of mystery. "But before we proceed, I must share something of great importance."

The villagers gathered around her, their eyes fixed on her every word.

"Within each of you lies a dormant power," Kaida continued, her voice soft yet commanding. "It is the strength of your love for this forest, the bond you share with its every creature, and the determination to protect it at all costs. This power, once awakened, can heal the deepest wounds and bring harmony back to the land."

Ling's heart fluttered with anticipation. He had sensed this dormant power within himself and the villagers. Now, with Kaida's guidance, he knew it was time to unlock it.

"Close your eyes," Kaida instructed, her voice carrying a soothing lilt. "Quiet your minds and envision the forest within you. Feel its heartbeat and let its energy flow through you."

With a collective breath, Ling and the villagers obeyed, plunging into a world of darkness behind their closed eyelids. Images of ancient trees, rushing rivers, and soaring birds flickered in their minds, intertwining their souls with the spirit of the forest.

As they focused on that connection, Ling felt a warmth growing within him. It radiated from his core, spreading like wildfire throughout his body. He knew that the same was happening to each villager standing beside him.

Opening his eyes, Ling witnessed a breathtaking sight. Light burst forth from each villager, creating an ethereal glow that surrounded them. It mingled with the forest's energy, shimmering with vibrant hues of green, gold, and azure.

Kaida's eyes gleamed with pride as she observed the villagers' transformation. "You have awakened the power within you," she said, her voice filled with awe. "Now, together, we shall harness this power and restore balance to the forest."

With a surge of energy coursing through their veins, Ling and the villagers moved forward, their steps lighter and purposeful. They were no longer just protectors; they were the embodiment of nature's strength and resilience.

As they advanced, a melody drifted through the air, carried by unseen hands. Ling recognized it as the song of the forest, a harmonious chorus of whispers that resonated deep within his being. It whispered tales of the forest's past and hopes for its future.

The enchanting melody blended with the villagers' newfound power, their collective voices rising in perfect harmony. Their words reverberated through the trees, awakening dormant creatures and rejuvenating the very essence of the forest.

Ling marveled at the sight unfolding before him plants and flowers regaining their vibrant colors, animals frolicking in the renewed serenity, and the once-dimmed light of the forest shining brighter than ever.

But Ling knew that their journey was far from over. The lurking darkness still awaited, clinging to the edges of the forest, threatening to extinguish their newfound triumph. With their awakened power, Ling and the villagers braced themselves for the challenges that lay ahead.

United by their shared purpose and the glowing energy within, they ventured deeper into the mystical realm, ready to confront whatever darkness awaited them. Together, they would protect the forest and ensure its everlasting splendor for generations to come.

And so, Ling and the villagers, fueled by the power of their love for the forest, pressed onward, ready to face the trials that awaited them. Their hearts ablaze with unwavering determination, they continued their journey, their spirits entwined with the magic of the wise monkey and the eternal wisdom of Kaida.

## Chapter 48

As the morning sun cast its golden rays upon the forest, Ling and his companions woke up to a world bathed in warmth and hope. The once somber atmosphere was replaced by a gentle breeze that whispered tales of new beginnings.

Ling looked around and saw Mei tending to the freshly planted saplings, her smile mirroring the delicate blossoms that adorned the trees. Sora sat nearby, his flute in hand, playing a tune that seemed to dance with the vibrant colors of the forest.

The children giggled as they chased after butterflies, their laughter echoing through the revitalized woods. Ling couldn't help but feel a twinge of joy in his heart, knowing that they had played a part in this transformation.

Kaida emerged from the shadows, her long silver hair shimmering in the sunlight. "This is only the beginning," she said, her voice carrying a sense of serene confidence. "As long as we stay united and protect the forest, it will continue to flourish."

Ling nodded, his eyes filled with determination. "We won't let anything harm our home again," he declared, his voice ringing with conviction.

Together, they walked along the familiar paths, observing the forest's gradual rejuvenation. Where once there was desolation, now there were sprouts of green, bursting with life. Ling marveled at the resilience of nature, its ability to heal and flourish even in the face of adversity.

As they ventured deeper into the forest, they stumbled upon a hidden glade, bathed in dappled sunlight. Flowers of every hue carpeted the ground, their sweet fragrance filling the air. Ling and the villagers couldn't help but lose themselves in the beauty that surrounded them.

"This place is magical," Mei whispered, her eyes sparkling with wonder.

Kaida nodded, a serene smile gracing her lips. "This glade is a sanctuary, a reminder of the enchantment that exists within the world. Nature has a way of teaching us to appreciate the simple joys in life."

Ling closed his eyes, feeling the warmth of the sunlight on his face. He breathed in deeply, taking in the earthy scent of the forest. At that moment, a weight seemed to lift from his shoulders, replaced by a renewed sense of purpose.

With each step they took, Ling and his companions carried hope within their hearts. They knew that the road ahead wouldn't be easy, but they were determined to protect their home and everything they held dear. The forest had taught them the power of unity, and they would forever be bound by their unwavering bond.

As the day drew to a close and the sun began its descent, Ling's heart swelled with a sense of gratitude. They had come a long way, and though the darkness still lingered on the horizon, he knew they would face it with courage and resilience.

The story of Ling, the wise monkey, was far from over. It was a tale of friendship, bravery, and the extraordinary power that lies within ordinary beings. Ling and his companions stood ready, ready to face whatever challenges awaited them, ready to protect the forest they called home.

And so, as the forest whispered its secrets and the stars emerged in the night sky, Ling knew that they were not alone. The universe had conspired to bring them together, to guide them on this extraordinary journey.

With hearts alight, they prepared for the next chapter, ready to embrace the unknown with unwavering determination and a glimmer of hope.

## Chapter 49

Ling and his companions continued their journey through the flourishing forest, their hearts filled with hope and determination. The sunlight filtered through the vibrant leaves, casting a warm glow upon the ground as they made their way deeper into the enchanted woods.

As they walked, Mei noticed a peculiar shimmer in the distance. Curiosity pulled them forward, and they quickened their pace. Soon, they arrived at a clearing where an ancient tree stood tall, its bark etched with mystical symbols.

"This must be the next step on our quest," Ling said, his eyes sparkling with anticipation. "We must unlock the wisdom of this wise old tree."

Sora stepped closer to the tree and gently placed a hand on its trunk. Suddenly, a surge of energy passed through her, causing her hair to stand on end. The tree's voice echoed in her mind.

"Only by facing the trials of the elements can you discover the true essence of harmony," the tree whispered, its voice as ancient as time itself.

The companions exchanged glances, understanding the tree's message. They needed to face the elements and prove their unyielding bond with nature to proceed.

With newfound determination, Ling, Mei, Sora, and the children set out to face the first trial, represented by fire. They followed the sound of crackling flames until they arrived at a clearing filled with flickering torches.

At the center of the clearing stood a fearsome creature, a fire spirit, its blazing red eyes scanning the group. The fire spirit's voice resounded through the air, crackling with intensity.

"To prove your worth, you must withstand the heat of the flames," the fire spirit declared. "Only those who embrace the fire within will be deemed worthy."

Without hesitation, Ling stepped forward, his

hands raised towards the heavens. He closed his eyes, channeling his inner strength, and a small flame materialized in his palm. Gently, he blew on the flame, causing it to grow.

The fire spirit observed him, its gaze penetrating. It circled Ling, flames dancing in its wake. The heat intensified, but Ling remained steadfast, his eyes reflecting the fiery determination within.

One by one, Mei, Sora, and the children followed Ling's example. Flames danced across their palms as they embraced the fire within, showing their unwavering spirit.

The fire spirit's eyes softened, and the flames surrounding them slowly dimmed. It emerged from the fire and transformed into a majestic phoenix with wings of golden fire.

"You have passed the first trial," the phoenix proclaimed, its voice now gentle and warm. "Your bond with fire is strong, and within you burns the flame of unity. Proceed with courage, for the path ahead is fraught with challenges."

As the phoenix disappeared into the sky, Ling and his companions smiled at one another, knowing that they were one step closer to unlocking the wisdom of the ancient tree. The fire had tested their strength, but they had emerged unscathed.

They pressed onward, the forest whispering tales of their courage and resilience. Ling's heart swelled with gratitude for the companionship and harmony they shared.

Little did they know that greater trials and revelations awaited them, but their spirits remained unwavering. Side by side, they continued their journey, ready to face whatever lay ahead and protect the forest, their beloved home, with all their might.

## Chapter 50

Ling and his companions, fueled by their recent triumph, ventured deeper into the heart of the enchanted forest. As they walked, the air grew cooler and the sounds of rustling leaves filled their ears. A hush fell over the group as they stumbled upon a clearing, where a glistening lake mirrored the sun's rays.

"This place feels magical," whispered Sora, her voice tinged with awe.

Ling nodded, his eyes sparkling with anticipation. The ancient tree's wisdom echoed in his mind, urging him to seek further enlightenment. He knew that the journey ahead held the key to understanding their ultimate purpose.

Kaida, their steadfast guide, led them toward the lake's edge. Ling placed his hand over the water and felt a current of energy surge through him. Ripples spread across the surface, reflecting their eager faces.

"The lake holds secrets," Ling declared. "Secrets we must uncover to protect the forest."

Mei's curiosity shone in her eyes. "But how do we unlock these secrets, Ling?"

Ling glanced at the others, a knowing smile playing on his lips. "We must embrace the power of the elements. Each of us possesses a unique bond with nature, and it is through this bond that we shall reveal the hidden wisdom."

Excitement surged through the group as Ling shared his insight. They were ready to face the challenges that awaited them, eager to prove their connection with the elements.

Ling stepped forward, his hand still in the water. He closed his eyes, focusing on the whispers of the wind. As he did, a gust of air swirled around him, lifting his robe and tousling his hair. His connection with the wind deepened, and he felt a surge of energy fill his entire being.

Next, Mei took her place beside Ling. She rooted herself to the ground, feeling the steady pulse of the earth beneath her feet. She closed her eyes, diving into the depths of her connection. The ground beneath her trembled gently, affirming her bond with the earth.

Sora stepped forward, raising her hands to the sky. She felt the warmth of the sun on her skin and the gentle caress of the rain in her hair. In her mind, she danced with the elements, harmonizing with the ever-changing weather.

The children, inspired by their companions, followed suit. They too embraced the elements, their young spirits intertwining with Ling, Mei, and Sora.

Together, the group channeled their collective energy, generating a powerful force that echoed through the clearing. The lake responded, its surface swirling and transforming into a vibrant kaleidoscope of colors.

And then, a figure materialized before them.

"Welcome, seekers of wisdom," a gentle voice resonated from the depths of the lake. "I am Aquila, the guardian of this sacred place."

Ling bowed respectfully. "We come seeking guidance, Aquila. We wish to protect our beloved forest from the darkness that threatens its existence."

Aquila's wise eyes studied each of them in turn. "The path you seek is one of unity, young ones. Only by embracing your bonds with nature and each other can you triumph over the looming darkness."

Ling and his companions listened intently, their hearts filled with determination. They knew that this encounter was yet another puzzle piece in their journey. They were ready to face whatever trials lay ahead, fueled by their unyielding spirit and unbreakable bond.

The stage was set, and the forest's fate hung in the balance. Their quest for wisdom and protection had only just begun, and it would require every ounce of their strength and unwavering belief.

But together, Ling and his companions knew they were capable of achieving the impossible.

## Chapter 51

Ling and his companions stood before Aquila, the majestic guardian of the sacred place. Her wings shimmered in shades of azure and emerald, reflecting the wisdom she held within. A gentle breeze rustled through the clearing, carrying a sense of anticipation.

With a regal nod, Aquila addressed the group. "To truly protect this forest, you must understand the delicate harmony that exists within it. The balance between light and darkness, growth and decay, creation and destruction."

Ling listened intently, his eyes fixed on Aquila's wise gaze. He knew that his journey had only just begun, and there was much more to learn.

Aquila continued her voice like a soothing melody. "I will guide you through the trials that will test your connection to nature and your determination to defend it. These trials will challenge your inner strength and forge an unbreakable bond with the forest."

Ling's heart swelled with determination, and he exchanged a knowing glance with Mei, Sora, and the children. They were ready to face whatever obstacles lay ahead, guided by Aquila's wisdom.

With a gentle sweep of her wings, Aquila led them to a hidden grove nestled within the enchanted forest. The grove was bathed in a soft, ethereal light, casting an otherworldly glow on the ancient trees that surrounded them.

"The Trial of Reflection awaits you here," Aquila explained, her voice resonating through the grove. "To truly understand nature, you must first understand yourselves."

Ling and his companions exchanged puzzled glances, unsure of the meaning behind Aquila's words. But they trusted in her guidance and were eager to uncover the depths of their connection to the forest.

As they stepped forward, the ancient trees began to shimmer, their bark transforming into reflective surfaces. Ling saw his reflection, but it was not the image of a monkey that stared back at him.

Instead, he saw himself as a guardian of the forest, his eyes filled with compassion and determination. Mei saw herself as a gentle breeze, carrying whispers of hope, while Sora saw herself as a beacon of light, guiding lost souls to safety.

The children saw their reflections too, envisioning themselves as the future protectors of this sacred place, their hearts brimming with love for nature.

The Trial of Reflection revealed their true essence, showing them the strength they possessed within their hearts. Ling understood that their bond with the forest ran deeper than he could have ever imagined.

Aquila watched with pride as they embraced their newfound identities, their reflection murmuring words of encouragement and unity. Ling and his companions had proved their unyielding connection to nature in the Trial of Reflection.

With a nod of approval, Aquila spoke, her voice filled with admiration. "You have passed this trial, young guardians. But remember, the journey ahead will not be without challenges. Stay true to yourselves and the guidance of the forest. Only then can you unlock the wisdom that lies within."

As Ling and his companions left the grove, their hearts were filled with a newfound sense of purpose. They knew that they were bound by an unbreakable bond, destined to protect the forest and its delicate balance.

With each step forward, Ling and his companions prepared themselves for the trials that awaited them, eager to face the darkness and bring light to the enchanted forest once more.

The journey had only just begun, and Ling knew that with unity, love, and the wisdom they would gain, they could overcome any obstacle that threatened their beloved home.

Together, they would become the guardians that the forest needed.

## Chapter 52

Ling and his companions stood at the entrance of the Trial of Courage, their hearts pounding with anticipation. Aquila had warned them that this trial would test their bravery and unwavering commitment to their cause.

As they entered the trial, the surroundings changed dramatically. No longer were they surrounded by vibrant greenery and calming streams. Instead, they found themselves in a dark and treacherous landscape, filled with towering cliffs and deep chasms. The wind howled ominously, carrying with it a sense of foreboding.

Ling glanced at Mei, Sora, and the children, their faces etched with determination. They had come so far, overcoming every obstacle in their path. Ling had faith that together they could conquer whatever challenges awaited them in the Trial of Courage.

The first test materialized before them as a narrow bridge, shrouded in darkness. It seemed to stretch endlessly across a vast void. Ling took a deep breath, leading the way with a torch in hand. Step by step, they cautiously made their way across the rickety bridge, their hearts pounding with every creak and sway.

The bridge shook violently beneath their feet, threatening to send them plummeting into the depths below. But Ling encouraged his companions to remain focused, assuring them they would prevail. Together, they forged ahead, their bonds growing stronger with each perilous step.

As they reached the end of the bridge, a roar echoed through the air. Ling turned to see a massive, fearsome creature blocking their path. Its fiery eyes glowed with malice, and its razor-sharp claws glinted menacingly.

Ling knew he had to face this creature head-on. With unwavering resolve, he stepped forward, summoning the wisdom and courage he had acquired through their journey. The creature lunged at Ling, but he swiftly dodged its attack, his agility honed by his time spent in the forest.

With each move, Ling fought with grace and precision. Mei, Sora, and the children watched in awe as their friend deftly evaded the creature's strikes. Ling's determination never wavered, and an unwavering connection with the forest seemed to flow through him, guiding his every action.

Finally, Ling delivered a decisive blow, striking the creature's vulnerable spot. With a mighty roar, the creature dissolved into a cloud of mist, dispersing into the night air. Ling stood triumphant, his heart filled with a mix of relief and satisfaction.

The path ahead cleared, revealing a radiant beam of light shining through the darkness. Ling and his companions walked towards it, their spirits lifted by their success. They knew that this trial had tested more than just their courage it had solidified their bonds and shown them the true extent of their strength.

The next trial awaited them, but Ling and his companions were ready. They had proven their valor and were prepared to face whatever challenges lay ahead. With the wisdom of the forest guiding them and their hearts brimming with determination, they would continue their mission to protect their beloved home.

And so, Ling and his companions ventured further into the Trial of Courage, their spirits unwavering, ready to overcome the obstacles that stood between them and the ultimate wisdom sought by the wise monkey.

## Chapter 53

Ling and his companions took a moment to catch their breath after conquering the treacherous Trial of Courage. As they stood on solid ground, surrounded by the whispering trees, a gentle breeze brushed against their faces, carrying with it a sense of anticipation.

Aquila, her eyes gleaming with pride, spoke with a voice that echoed through the forest. "You have proven your courage, my friends. But the journey to unlock the wisdom of the ancient tree is not yet complete. The Trial of Wisdom awaits."

The companions exchanged glances, their hearts filled with equal parts excitement and nervousness. Ling, his fur standing on end, knew that the trial ahead was unlike any they had faced before. The very idea of unraveling the complexities of wisdom seemed daunting.

Aquila, sensing their concern, reassured them

with a gentle smile. "Wisdom is not simply found in books or knowledge. It resides within the bonds you share, the lessons you have learned, and the love you have for the forest. Trust in yourselves and the way forward will reveal itself."

With determination fueling their spirits, the companions pressed on. They followed Aquila's guidance through the dense foliage until they stumbled upon an ancient amphitheater nestled in a clearing. Moss-covered stone benches encircled a raised platform, upon which the grandest of trees stood tall.

Ling and his friends approached the tree, its gnarled branches reaching out like arms, beckoning them closer. As they drew near, the tree emitted a warm, golden glow, illuminating their faces with a soft radiance.

A voice, rich and wise, infused the air around them. "To unlock the wisdom within, you must reveal your true selves. Each of you, step forward and share the lessons you have learned."

Ling swallowed hard, his heart pounding in his chest. He stepped forward first, the weight of responsibility heavy on his shoulders. "I have learned that true strength lies not in physical might, but in the bonds we forge and the unity we embrace."

Mei, her eyes shining with determination, stepped forward next. "I have learned the importance of bravery and facing our fears head on. Only by confronting what scares us can we find the strength to protect what we hold dear."

Sora, her voice steady with conviction, took her place beside Mei. "I have learned the power of empathy and understanding. By embracing the perspectives of others, we can build bridges and inspire change."

The children, their eyes bright with innocent wisdom, stood together, their voices blending as one. "We have learned that small actions can make a big difference. Even the tiniest seed can grow into a mighty tree."

The ancient tree's branches quivered and rustled as if nodding in approval. The golden glow intensified, enveloping Ling and his companions in a warm embrace. At that moment, they felt a surge of knowledge and understanding flow through their veins, connecting them to the wisdom of the forest itself.

As the glow subsided, Aquila stepped forward, a twinkle in her eye. "You have passed the Trial of Wisdom, my friends. The forest recognizes your worthiness and grants you its eternal guidance."

Ling and his companions exchanged glances, their hearts brimming with gratitude. They knew that together, armed with wisdom and unity, they were prepared to face whatever challenges lay ahead.

With renewed determination, they turned their gaze toward the unknown, ready to protect the forest and all its inhabitants with the depth of their newfound wisdom.

## Chapter 54

Ling and his companions, filled with newfound wisdom, ventured further into the depths of the enchanted forest. The air was thick with anticipation as they followed the winding path, the trees whispering secrets only they could hear. The forest seemed to pulsate with an ancient energy, guiding them towards their next trial.

As they approached a clearing bathed in golden sunlight, a gentle voice echoed through the air. "Welcome, brave travelers," it whispered, and the group turned to find an ethereal figure floating above them. It was Master Tsubasa, the ancient sage rumored to possess infinite knowledge.

Ling and his companions bowed respectfully, their hearts pounding with excitement. Master Tsubasa's eyes sparkled with wisdom as he spoke, "You have come seeking knowledge, young ones. The Trial of Wisdom awaits you, where your minds will be tested and your choices will shape the fate of the forest."

Curiosity burned within their hearts as they listened attentively. Master Tsubasa continued, "In this trial, you shall encounter three puzzles that will challenge your intellect. Listen closely, for only the wise can overcome these tests and unlock the vast wisdom of the forest."

With determined expressions, Ling and his companions followed Master Tsubasa deeper into the clearing. The first puzzle, framed by towering columns, stood before them. A riddle carved into a stone slab awaited their scrutiny.

"Two sisters, born the same day, but not twins. One dances in the daylight, while the other fades when the sun sets. Who are they?"

The companions exchanged puzzled glances, their minds whirling with possibilities. Ling's eyes gleamed, and he whispered, "Day and Night, for they are sisters entwined in an eternal dance."

A soft hum resonated in the air, and the columns shifted, revealing a path forward. Ling's companions marveled at his wisdom, knowing that they were truly in the presence of a wise monkey.

As they moved deeper into the trial, the second puzzle awaited them. A mosaic, crafted from colorful stones, depicted various animals coexisting in perfect harmony. Above it loomed a question.

"In the circle of life, who weaves the tapestry of balance and unity?"

Each member of the group pondered the question, their gazes sweeping across the mosaic. Suddenly, Isha, the wise owl, spoke with certainty, "It is Nature itself, the weaver of balance and unity."

A gentle breeze rustled the leaves, and the mosaic shimmered, opening a passage to the final challenge. Ling's companions marveled at Isha's insight, knowing that they were all part of a harmonious tapestry woven by nature's hands.

As they approached the third and final puzzle, anticipation filled the air. Engraved on a stone pedestal was a profound question, demanding their utmost contemplation.

"What is the greatest power in the world, capable of both destruction and creation, yet forever seeking harmony?"

Ling and his companions huddled together, their eyes locked in deep thought. After a moment, Kaida, the steadfast fox, spoke confidently, "It is Love, for its power can reshape the world, bringing both chaos and harmony."

A resounding melody filled the air, and the stone pedestal sank into the ground, revealing a radiant doorway leading to the heart of the forest.

Ling and his companions exchanged triumphant smiles, their hearts swelling with pride. They had proven their wisdom and earned the right to unlock the eternal guidance of the forest. United, they stepped through the doorway, prepared to face the next trials that awaited them and protect their beloved home.

Little did they know that their journey was far from over, for greater challenges lay ahead, and the fate of the forest would ultimately rest upon their shoulders.

## Chapter 55

In the heart of the enchanted forest, Ling and his companions stood before a towering waterfall. Its cascading waters shimmered under the warm sunlight, creating a rainbow of vibrant colors. Ling marveled at the sight, feeling a sense of awe and wonder fill his being.

Master Tsubasa, with his long white beard and wise eyes, approached the group. "This is the Trial of Intuition," he explained, his voice steady and filled with ancient wisdom. "To proceed, you must trust your instincts and follow the path that speaks to your heart."

Ling and his companions exchanged glances, anticipation buzzing in the air. They knew they had grown as individuals and as a team throughout their journey, but this trial would test their ability to listen to their inner voice.

As they stepped closer to the waterfall, a mystical mist enveloped them, swirling around their forms. Ling closed his eyes, emptying his mind and focusing on the sound of rushing water.

Suddenly, Ling's ears caught a faint melody carried by the wind. The soft notes beckoned him to follow, resonating deep within his heart. Without hesitation, he stepped onto a hidden path beside the waterfall, his companions following closely behind.

The path led them through a dense thicket adorned with vibrant flowers. The air smelled sweet, and the gentle rustling of leaves provided a soothing melody as they walked. Ling trusted his intuition, confident that their destination drew nearer with each step.

They emerged into a serene clearing, surrounded by ancient trees with intertwined branches, forming a natural canopy overhead. Sunlight filtered through the intricate patterns created by the leaves, casting a warm glow on their faces.

In the center of the clearing stood a colossal tree, its trunk lined with moss and its branches reaching for the heavens. Ling felt an overwhelming sense of reverence as if the tree held the collective wisdom of the forest within its ancient core.

As they approached the tree, Ling noticed intricate carvings etched onto its bark, depicting various animals and symbols. It was a language unique to the forest, a language of nature and wisdom.

With bated breath, Ling gently traced his fingers along the carvings, feeling the energy pulsate beneath his touch. The forest whispered its secrets to him, guiding him to decipher the hidden messages within the intricate carvings.

Ling's companions joined him, their fingers tracing the carvings as well. Together, they unraveled the ancient language, each symbol revealing a piece of the forest's eternal guidance.

Their intuition had led them to this pivotal moment, where they embraced the profound wisdom housed within the sacred tree. Ling knew that this knowledge would equip them for the greater challenges that lay ahead.

As the sun began its descent, casting an ethereal glow over the clearing, Ling and his companions sat in a circle beneath the majestic tree. They listened to the forest's whispered guidance, absorbing its teachings like sponges.

The Trial of Intuition had tested their ability to trust themselves and one another. Ling marveled at the bond they had forged, their collective intuition intertwining like the roots of the ancient tree before them.

With the eternal guidance of the forest embedded within their hearts, Ling and his companions prepared to face the trials yet to come. There was no doubt in their minds that they were destined to protect the forest, to ensure its beauty and magic thrived for generations to come.

Their journey was far from over, and Ling's determination burned brighter than ever. The wise monkey and his companions were ready to embrace the challenges, armed with the wisdom and intuition bestowed upon them by the enchanted forest.

## Chapter 56

In the depths of the enchanted forest, Ling and his companions continued their journey, their hearts filled with anticipation. The whispering trees rustled as the wind carried their ancient secrets, guiding the group deeper into the unknown.

As they ventured further, the air grew thick with a sense of mystery, and a soft glow illuminated the path ahead. Ling's keen eyes caught a flicker of movement, causing him to pause. A figure emerged from the shadows, its silhouette shrouded in the ethereal light.

It was a girl, no older than Ling himself, with flowing silver hair that cascaded down her shoulders. Her eyes, as bright as moonlit stars, held a wisdom that seemed beyond her years. Ling was captivated by her presence as she gracefully approached the group.

"Welcome, wanderers of the forest," her voice

resonated like a gentle melody. "I am Mei, the guardian of the hidden truths that lie within this realm."

Ling and his companions exchanged curious glances, their hearts brimming with questions. How had Mei come to be in the enchanted forest? What secrets did she hold?

Feeling their curiosity, Mei smiled knowingly, sensing their unspoken thoughts. "I have been here for ages, immersing myself in the wisdom of this magical place. The ancient trees have entrusted me with their knowledge, and now, I shall share it with you."

Ling's companions leaned in closer, their eyes wide with anticipation. Mei continued, her voice soothing yet filled with authority.

"The enchanted forest is not only a sanctuary but a symbol of unity. It welcomes all who seek harmony with nature, for it understands the innate connection between humans and the world around them. Many have lost sight of their responsibilities, but I believe in the power of rediscovery."

She paused, scanning Ling and his companions with a discerning gaze. "Your presence here is no coincidence. It is fate that has brought us together."

Ling's heart pounded in his chest as he listened intently. Mei's words resonated within him, igniting a flicker of hope for the future.

"I sense your unwavering determination, your fierce loyalty to this forest," Mei continued. "But together, we can achieve so much more. With your courage and my guidance, we can rally the villages beyond these woods and protect the sanctity of this magical realm."

Ling and his companions exchanged glances, their expressions filled with newfound determination. Ling stepped forward, his voice filled with conviction.

"We have seen the destruction that humans can bring, but we have also witnessed the resilience and compassion they possess," Ling said. "With Mei's guidance and our united efforts, we can bridge the gap between our world and theirs."

Mei's eyes gleamed with approval. "It is time to reveal the hidden truths, the forgotten tales of the enchanted forest. Ling, I believe you hold the key to unlocking the villagers' hearts. Together, we shall restore the balance that has been disturbed."

Ling and his companions nodded in agreement, their spirits alight with a renewed sense of purpose. The journey that had begun as a mission to protect the forest had now expanded into something greater a mission to bridge the divide between humans and nature, to restore harmony where it had been lost.

With Mei by their side, Ling and his companions set forth, ready to face the challenges that awaited them. Unlikely allies bonded by their shared quest, they embarked on a new chapter, guided by the wisdom of the enchanted forest and fueled by the hope of a brighter future.

## Chapter 57

Ling and his companions, accompanied by Mei, ventured deeper into the enchanted forest. The air was thick with tranquility, and the whispering leaves added a sense of mystique to their journey. As they walked, Ling noticed something peculiar up ahead, a peculiar-looking tree with bright purple leaves and a mischievous grin etched into its bark.

Intrigued, Ling approached the tree cautiously, studying its peculiar face. "My friends," Ling called out, "come and see this!"

Curiosity piqued, his companions hurried over. Mei's eyes widened with disbelief as she saw the tree's comical expression. "Oh, how extraordinary! A laughing tree!"

Their gazes met, and a moment of silent understanding passed between them. Ling, never one to resist a good laugh, decided to test the tree's sense of humor.

With a mischievous glint in his eye, Ling whispered a silly joke into the tree's ear. The tree's bark began to tremble, and then, unexpectedly, it burst into uproarious laughter. Its branches swayed and shook, causing leaves to fall like confetti.

Ling's companions couldn't help but chuckle along, caught up in the infectious mirth of the enchanted tree. Mei joined in too, her laughter ringing through the forest, blending with the cheerful melody of nature.

As their laughter echoed through the trees, Ling couldn't help but feel a lightness in his heart. Amidst their mission to save the forest, this joyful mishap reminded them to find joy and laughter even in the darkest moments.

But their laughter didn't go unnoticed. From the corners of the forest, a group of squirrels, birds, and deer emerged, captivated by the jubilant spectacle. Ling and his companions found themselves at the center of a joyous gathering, as the animals joined their laughter, hopping and prancing in delight.

For a while, all worries dissolved into the mirthful atmosphere. Ling marveled at the power of laughter, how it could bring creatures together, forging bonds of joy and camaraderie. It was a reminder that even in the face of adversity, happiness could be found.

Eventually, their laughter subsided, and the

animals bid Ling and his companions farewell, disappearing back into the forest. Ling knew that their connection had deepened, and their resolve to protect the enchanted forest had grown stronger.

As they continued their journey, Ling couldn't help but smile, knowing that the forest had a way of teaching valuable lessons in the most unexpected and amusing ways. Ling and his companions pressed on, ready to face whatever challenges lay ahead, armed not only with wisdom but with laughter as well.

## Chapter 58

As the animals reveled in laughter and joy, Ling and his companions continued their journey through the enchanted forest. Mei guided them along the winding path, her footsteps light and graceful. The air carried a sense of anticipation, the scent of blooming flowers filling their senses.

They soon arrived at the edge of a dense thicket, where Mei paused and turned to face Ling and his companions. Her eyes sparkled with a mix of determination and mystery.

"Beyond this thicket lies the Hidden Lake," Mei whispered, her voice carrying a sense of reverence. "Legends say that the lake possesses the power to reveal hidden truths."

Ling and his companions exchanged intrigued glances, their curiosity piqued. Ling's heart raced with excitement, his intuition telling him that the Hidden Lake held the key to their mission.

Together, they pushed through the thicket, and their eyes widened in awe at the sight before them. A pristine lake, shimmering in iridescent hues, stretched out beneath the golden rays of the sun. The water seemed to hold a secret energy, an ancient wisdom whispering through the gentle ripples.

Ling approached the water's edge, the cool mist caressing his fur. He dipped his paw into the lake, and a tingling sensation traveled up his arm, sending shivers down his spine. Images, like snippets from forgotten dreams, flickered before his eyes.

He saw humans and animals living in harmony, dancing beneath moonlit skies. He witnessed the whispers of wind carrying the laughter of children, as they played among the ancient trees. Ling's heart swelled with hope and determination as he realized the hidden truths the Hidden Lake had unveiled.

Turning to his companions, Ling shared his revelations, his voice filled with conviction. "The Hidden Lake has shown us the forgotten bond between humans and nature. We must spread this wisdom and restore harmony to our world."

His words resonated deeply with Mei and the others. Their eyes gleamed with newfound purpose as they pledged to carry the message of unity beyond the enchanted forest.

As they prepared to leave the Hidden Lake, Mei approached Ling, her voice soft but resolute.

"Ling, the wise monkey," she began, her eyes reflecting the wisdom of the ages. "You possess a rare gift, the ability to bridge the gap between humans and nature. We will need your guidance to awaken the hearts of those who have forgotten."

Ling nodded, a sense of responsibility settling within him. He understood that his journey had only just begun and that the task ahead would be daunting. But with the support of Mei and his companions, Ling knew he could face any challenge that lay before him.

They set off once more, their spirits renewed by the Hidden Lake's revelations. Ling and his companions were ready to bring about change, to ignite the spark of harmony, and to protect the enchanted forest from further harm.

Little did they know that their united efforts would lead them to face their greatest trial yet, a test of courage and unwavering determination. Ling and his companions pressed on, their hearts ablaze with hope, ready to face whatever awaited them on their quest to restore balance and protect the mystical realm they held dear.

## Chapter 59

As Ling and his companions stood by the tranquil Hidden Lake, a rustling sound caught their attention. They turned towards the source, their eyes widening in surprise. Emerging from the thick foliage was a creature unlike any they had seen before.

It was a slender white fox, its fur shimmering under the dappled sunlight that filtered through the leaves. Its piercing blue eyes sparkled with an otherworldly glow, and as it approached, Ling felt a wave of magic in the air.

"Who are you?" Mei asked in awe, her voice barely more than a whisper.

The fox tilted its head and spoke with a voice that seemed to echo, "I am Amara, the guardian of the Enchanted Forest."

Ling felt a strange connection with Amara as if they shared a common purpose. "Amara, what brings you here?" he asked, his voice filled with curiosity.

The fox's eyes glimmered with ancient wisdom. "I sensed a great power within you, Ling," it replied. "The ancient language of the forest has chosen you as its vessel, its voice of guidance and protection."

Ling's heart swelled with pride, understanding the immense responsibility that lay upon his furry shoulders. "But what does this mean?" he asked, searching for clarity.

Amara approached Ling, its delicate nose lightly touching his whiskers. "The power within you can unite humans and nature," Amara explained. "But it also attracts those who wish to exploit it for their gain."

Ling's companions exchanged worried glances, realizing the grave danger that awaited them. They knew that their mission to protect the forest had only just begun.

"But fear not," Amara reassured them, its voice soothing. "With the strength of your bond and the wisdom of the forest, you can overcome any obstacle. Ling, you are not alone in this journey. Together with your friends and the enchanted creatures of this forest, you will triumph."

Ling and his companions felt a renewed sense of purpose. They knew that the road ahead would be treacherous, filled with challenges and unknown dangers. But they also understood that their mission was greater than themselves it was about preserving the delicate balance of nature and showing humans the beauty and wisdom that lay within it.

As Amara faded back into the forest, Ling and his companions shared a determined look. They would face whatever lay ahead with courage, knowing that the power of their unity and the wisdom of the enchanted forest would guide them.

The adventure continued, and as the sun began to set, casting a golden glow over the hidden lake, Ling and his companions set off deeper into the heart of the Enchanted Forest. With each step they took, they carried the hope of harmony between humans and nature, vowing to protect the world they held so dear.

## Chapter 60

Ling, Mei, Sora, and Amara stood at the edge of the Hidden Lake, mesmerized by its tranquil beauty. The water shimmered with an ethereal glow as if holding the secrets of the forest within its depths. Surrounding the lake were towering trees, their leaves whispering ancient tales that only the wind could decipher.

Amara, the mystical white fox, led the group towards the heart of the forest, where they would meet the Council of Elders an assembly of wise creatures who held the key to restoring harmony between humans and nature.

As they ventured deeper into the enchanted forest, Ling could feel a new energy pulsating through his veins. It was as if the forest itself had chosen him to be its guardian. Ling marveled at the responsibility bestowed upon him, realizing that his actions would shape the fate of the magical realm.

The forest grew denser, the sunlight peeking through the canopy above casting dappled shadows on the path. Ling could hear the whispers of the trees, guiding them towards their destination. The group moved with a renewed sense of purpose, following the chorus of whispers weaving through the air.

Finally, they arrived at a clearing bathed in a soft golden light. In the center stood a great tree, its branches reaching towards the heavens like outstretched arms. The Council of Elders awaited them, a gathering of majestic creatures the wise old owl, the graceful deer, the gentle river spirit, and others with wisdom etched into their ancient eyes.

Ling felt a mixture of awe and humility as he approached the Council. He knew that they held the answers they sought, the knowledge necessary to mend the bond between humans and nature.

The wise owl, perched on a branch, looked at Ling with penetrating eyes. "Ling, you have been chosen by the forest to carry its wisdom within you," the owl spoke, its voice a soothing melody in Ling's ears. "You must seek the path of unity, for it is through understanding that the balance between humans and nature can be restored."

Mei stepped forward, her eyes shimmering with determination. "But how do we bridge the gap between humans and nature? How can we make them understand the importance of preserving this magical realm?"

The graceful deer stepped forward, its antlers adorned with delicate flowers. "It is through storytelling and compassion that the hearts of humans can be touched," the deer replied. "By sharing the tales of the enchanted forest and awakening a sense of wonder and reverence within them, we can ignite a spark of change."

Sora, the cunning fox, nodded with understanding. "We must unite the villagers and the creatures of the forest, showing them that they are not adversaries but allies," Sora said. "Together, we can protect this realm and create a harmonious bond that will withstand the test of time."

Ling felt a surge of determination, a fire burning within him. He knew that the journey ahead would not be easy, but he also knew that their cause was worth fighting for. Ling, Mei, Sora, and Amara made a vow then and there, pledging to carry the wisdom of the enchanted forest far and wide.

As the sun dipped below the horizon, the Council of Elders bestowed upon Ling a sacred pendant a symbol of their trust and belief in him. Ling wore it proudly around his neck, knowing that it carried the weight of their hopes and dreams.

With the guidance of Mei, the wisdom of the Council, and the unbreakable bond between Ling and his companions, they set forth on their mission. Their journey would be filled with challenges, but Ling was ready to face them head-on, for he knew that the fate of the enchanted forest depended on their efforts.

And so, Ling, Mei, Sora, and Amara embarked on their grand adventure, their hearts filled with a resolute purpose. They would walk hand in paw, united and steadfast, spreading the whispers of harmony and protecting the secrets of the magical realm.

## Chapter 61

The once vibrant forest now bore a darker hue, as shadows cast their ominous presence over the enchanted realm. Ling and his companions, Mei, Sora, and Amara, could sense a growing unease deep within their hearts.

As they journeyed further, the air became heavy, filled with a foreboding stillness that sent shivers down their spines. The whispering leaves that used to share secrets now seemed to hiss with doubt and uncertainty. Ling's wise eyes searched for answers, but even the ancient trees remained silent, their branches swaying with trepidation.

The Council of Elders, a group of wise and ancient creatures, awaited their arrival in a secluded grove at the heart of the forest. Ling, Mei, Sora, and Amara cautiously approached, their hearts heavy with worry.

The Elders, normally serene and composed,

appeared troubled. Their fur and feathers were ruffled, and their eyes reflected a deep sadness. Ling could see the weight of their wisdom etched upon their faces as if the burden of protecting the magical realm had become too great.

"We have called upon you, the guardians of our realm," a wise old owl spoke, his voice tinged with sorrow. "For the harmony we vowed to protect is crumbling before our eyes."

Ling's heart sank as he listened to the Elders recount tales of the forest's gradual decline. Humans, driven by greed and ignorance, began encroaching further into the enchanted realm, felling trees and disturbing the delicate balance that Ling and his companions fought so hard to restore.

"We have lost touch with the humans, our once sacred bond severed," an ancient stag added mournfully. "Our attempts to unite them with nature have been met with hostility and indifference."

The weight of their words bore heavily upon Ling's shoulders. His mission to bridge the gap between humans and nature suddenly felt insurmountable. Doubt gnawed at his core, questioning if he was truly worthy of this immense responsibility.

Mei's gentle voice broke through Ling's turmoil. "We have come so far, Ling. We mustn't let despair consume us. Our bond with nature and the wisdom we carry have the power to guide us through even the darkest times."

Sora, the bold and courageous rabbit, spoke up, "Let us rally the creatures of the forest, and remind them of their purpose. Together, we can reignite the flame of hope within each heart."

Amara, her eyes shimmering with determination, added, "The path ahead may be treacherous, but we have each other and the wisdom of the enchanted forest to light our way. We will not falter."

Ling took in the steadfast resolve of his companions, drawing strength from their unwavering faith. The darkness may have encroached upon the forest, but he knew that deep within, the spark of harmony still flickered. With renewed determination, he vowed to protect that flickering light until it blazed once more, illuminating the path toward a brighter future.

As they left the somber grove, Ling, Mei, Sora, and Amara embarked on a new phase of their mission to rekindle hope and inspire others to join their cause. The road ahead was fraught with challenges, but Ling knew that as long as they remained true to the wisdom they carried within, the enchanted forest would find its way back to harmony.

## Chapter 62

Ling stood before the Council of Elders, his heart pounding with a mix of fear and determination. The wise animals gathered around him, their ancient eyes filled with wisdom and concern. The forest, once vibrant and full of life, had started to wither under the weight of human encroachment.

"We have seen the darkness creeping into our once lively realm," one of the elders murmured, her voice filled with sorrow. "The balance between humans and nature is tipping, and we fear for our home."

Ling felt a heavy weight settle on his shoulders as he looked at his companions. Mei, Sora, and Amara stood beside him, their eyes filled with trust. They believed in him, in his ability to bridge the gap between humans and nature. But now, faced with the council's somber words, Ling doubted himself.

"What would you have me do?" Ling asked, his voice filled with both uncertainty and determination.

The eldest of the council, a wise owl with silver feathers, hopped forward and gazed into Ling's eyes. "You are the chosen one, Ling," the owl said, his voice like a gentle breeze. "The forest chose you for a reason. You possess the wisdom and compassion to heal this world."

Ling felt a glimmer of hope ignited within him. The council's words started to sink in, seeping into his heart like the nourishing rain. He was not alone in this battle. He had the support of the council, his companions, and the enchanted realm itself.

"Tell me," Ling said, his voice steadier now. "What can I do to restore harmony?"

The council murmured amongst themselves, their ancient voices blending like a symphony. Finally, the eldest owl spoke again. "You must journey beyond the enchanted forest, to the realm of humans. There, you will find the ones who still hold the spark of connection to nature within their hearts. Nurture that spark, and help them understand the importance of preserving our home."

Ling nodded, feeling the weight on his shoulders shift. He was ready to face the world beyond the forest, armed with the wisdom of the enchanted realm. Ling turned to Mei, Sora, and Amara, determination shining in his eyes.

"We will embark on this journey together," Ling declared, his voice filled with conviction. "We will find those who still yearn for harmony, and together, we will protect this realm."

With renewed purpose, Ling and his companions set forth from the heart of the enchanted forest. They ventured into the unknown, guided by the whispers of the wind and the steady beat of their united hearts. Ling knew it wouldn't be an easy path, but he also knew that within his paw, the power to change the world lay.

As they disappeared into the dappled shadows of the forest, Ling held on to the council's words, their wisdom etched into his very being. He was ready to become the bridge between humans and nature, to make the world aware of the fragile beauty that lay within the enchanted realm. And with every step he took, Ling drew strength from the love and dedication of his companions, knowing that together, they would bring harmony back to both realms.

## Chapter 63

Ling and his companions ventured deeper into the enchanted forest, their footsteps muffled by the thick carpet of moss beneath their feet. The air hung heavy with anticipation, a mix of excitement and trepidation swirling within them. They were on a mission to restore the harmony between humans and nature, but they needed guidance and a spark of hope to fuel their journey.

As they stepped into a small clearing, a gentle breeze rustled the leaves overhead, and Ling caught a glimpse of movement out of the corner of his eye. He turned his head, his heart skipping a beat, and saw a figure emerging from the shadows.

The figure was tall and slender, cloaked in a flowing, moss-green robe that seemed to blend seamlessly with the forest. Their face was hidden beneath a hood, revealing only a pair of sparkling emerald eyes that shone with otherworldly wisdom. Ling felt a strange connection as if he had known this person before, in another time and place.

"Who are you?" Ling asked, his voice quivering with curiosity.

The figure stepped forward, their presence radiating a calm and mysterious energy. "I am the Wanderer," they replied, their voice soft and melodious like a gentle river. "I have traveled through the realms, seeking those who hold the key to change."

Ling and his companions exchanged glances, their eyes filled with wonder and intrigue. Mei spoke up, her voice laced with excitement. "What key are you talking about? How can we bring harmony back to the enchanted forest?"

The Wanderer smiled, the corners of their lips curling up like the delicate petals of a flower. "The key lies within each of you," they answered cryptically. "It resides in your hearts, beckoning you to embrace your inner strength and trust in the wisdom you possess."

Sora furrowed his brow, a question burning in his eyes. "But how do we unlock this key? How do we restore the balance between humans and nature?"

The Wanderer raised a hand, and a soft, pulsating glow began to emanate from their palm. "Challenges are awaiting you, trials that will test your courage and determination," they said, their voice resonating deep within Ling's soul. "Only by facing these trials with unwavering conviction can you unlock the key and bring about the change you seek."

Ling stepped forward, his heart pounding in his chest. "We are ready," he declared, his voice filled with newfound determination. "Lead us to the trials, Wanderer. We will face them head-on and restore the harmony of this enchanted realm."

The Wanderer nodded, their emerald eyes gleaming with approval. "Follow me, young ones," they said, their voice filled with ancient knowledge. "We shall embark on a journey that will test your bonds, your resilience, and your belief in the power of unity."

And so, Ling, Mei, Sora, and their new companion, the enigmatic Wanderer, set forth into the depths of the enchanted forest. They knew that the trials ahead would be arduous, but with their unwavering determination and the wisdom they had gathered along their journey, they were ready to face whatever challenges awaited them.

Little did they know that these trials would reveal secrets long forgotten, ignite the dormant magic within them, and ultimately prove that the power to bridge the gap between humans and nature lay not in a single individual, but in the unity and collective spirit of all.

## Chapter 64

Ling, Mei, Sora, and Amara followed the Wanderer through a narrow path that wound its way deeper into the heart of the enchanted forest. The air grew thick with anticipation, and Ling could feel the weight of the forest's fate resting heavily on his shoulders. Questions swirled in his mind like leaves caught in a gust of wind.

As the group walked in silence, a sense of tranquility settled over them. Shafts of dappled sunlight pierced through the dense canopy above, casting ethereal patterns on the forest floor. Ling marveled at the play of light and shadow, reminded once again of nature's delicate balance.

Amara took the lead, guiding them to a tranquil grove where a crystal-clear pool shimmered under the gentle sway of weeping willows. The Wanderer gestured for Ling and his companions to sit around the pool and closed their eyes.

"Within this journey, you will face your inner selves," the Wanderer's voice resonated in Ling's mind. "To restore harmony between humans and nature, you must confront your fears, doubts, and desires."

Ling felt a twinge of trepidation, but he took a deep breath and allowed himself to surrender to the journey. Soon, vivid visions danced across his closed eyelids.

In his vision, Ling saw himself as a young boy, chasing butterflies in a meadow. The warmth of the sun on his face, the joy in his heart... It felt like a distant memory. Suddenly, the scene changed, and Ling found himself surrounded by barren land, and dark clouds overhead. Despair settled deep within his being, and the weight of his doubts threatened to drown him.

But just as Ling was about to succumb to the darkness, a flicker of light appeared. It grew brighter, revealing glimpses of the villagers, Mei, Sora, and Amara, all united in their determination to protect the forest. Ling realized that he was not alone, and strength surged through his veins.

The vision shifted again, and Ling found himself standing before a towering tree, its branches reaching for the sky. The tree whispered ancient secrets, sharing knowledge and wisdom with him. Ling listened intently, absorbing every word, feeling a profound connection to the forest.

When the visions ceased, Ling opened his eyes to see his companions sitting around him, their faces mirroring a mix of emotions: determination, vulnerability, and hope. Ling felt a newfound clarity within himself, knowing that their journey had only just begun.

"We must strive to see the beauty and value in both nature and humanity," Ling said, his voice resolute with determination. "Only by understanding and bridging the gap between the two can we restore harmony."

His companions nodded in agreement, their eyes filled with renewed purpose. Ling realized that their journey would require them to look inward, confront their shortcomings, and learn from them. They would need to inspire others to embrace the wisdom of the enchanted realm, to ignite a spark of change.

Together, Ling, Mei, Sora, and Amara rose from the tranquil grove, ready to face the challenges that lay ahead. The enchanted forest had entrusted them with a sacred task, and they would not falter in their mission.

With their hearts filled with courage and determination, they set forth into the unknown, ready to overcome any obstacle that stood in their way. Ling knew that the path ahead would be arduous, but he also knew that their collective strength and unwavering belief would guide them toward a future where humans and nature could harmoniously coexist.

And so, their journey of reflection continued, as Ling and his companions ventured deeper into the enchanted forest, embarking on a path that would forever change their lives and the fate of the world they held dear.

## Chapter 65

As Ling, Mei, Sora, and Amara meditated in the tranquil pool, a gentle breeze rustled the leaves above them. The air was thick with anticipation, and they all felt a sense of urgency pulsating through their veins. Their hearts beat in sync as they delved deeper into their journey of reflection.

Suddenly, a low growl shattered the peaceful atmosphere. Ling's eyes snapped open, and he sprang to his feet, alert and ready. Mei, Sora, and Amara followed suit, searching for the source of the disturbance.

Out of the shadows emerged a creature they had never encountered before an ethereal unicorn with shimmering silver fur and a majestic horn that glowed with a radiant light. Its eyes gleamed with wisdom and an ancient knowledge that seemed to transcend time itself.

The unicorn stepped gracefully toward Ling

and bowed its head in a sign of respect. Its voice resonated like a gentle whisper in the wind, carrying an air of both strength and vulnerability. "Greetings, brave travelers. I am Celestia, the guardian of the enchanted realm. I have awaited your arrival."

Ling's breath caught in his throat. "Celestia... we have heard stories of you. We seek your guidance to restore harmony between humans and nature," he said, his voice filled with reverence.

Celestia's eyes softened, and she nodded. "The harmony you seek can only be found by embracing the connection within yourselves. But beware, young ones, for the path you tread is one of great trials and challenges. The forces that threaten this harmony are formidable, and not all may be as they seem."

Mei stepped forward, her eyes gleaming with determination. "We are ready, Celestia. We will face whatever lies ahead to protect our world."

Sora and Amara nodded in agreement, their resolve unyielding. They had come too far to back down now.

Celestia's gaze lingered on Ling, her ancient

wisdom piercing through his soul. "Ling, the weight of this mission rests upon your shoulders. Your destiny is entwined with that of the enchanted realm."

Ling's heart raced, and a surge of doubt washed over him. He had always believed in the power of unity, but now, facing the enormity of his task, he felt the weight of responsibility. Could he truly bridge the gap between humans and nature?

Before he could voice his uncertainties, Celestia touched his forehead gently with her horn. A surge of energy coursed through Ling's body, infusing him with newfound confidence and an unshakeable belief in his purpose.

"As long as you remain true to your heart, Ling, the way will reveal itself," Celestia whispered, her voice filled with unwavering faith.

With Celestia's guidance, Ling and his companions embarked on a journey like no other. They traveled through treacherous landscapes, faced formidable adversaries, and encountered unexpected allies. Each trial they overcame deepened their understanding of the delicate balance between humans and nature.

As they ventured forth, Ling's doubts began to fade, replaced by a steadfast resolve to unite their world in harmony. With every step, they grew stronger, their bond as solid as the ancient trees of the enchanted forest.

The road ahead was unknown, and the challenges they would face were yet to be revealed. But with Celestia's guidance and the unwavering spirit within their hearts, they were prepared to face the unforeseen and restore the harmony that had been lost.

Little did they know, the greatest test of their journey awaited them, eager to challenge their resolve and set their destiny in motion.

## Chapter 66

Ling, Mei, Sora, Amara, and Celestia stood before the majestic unicorn, her silver mane shimmering in the sunlight. Her voice echoed with a sense of ancient wisdom as she spoke.

"The path you seek is not an easy one," Celestia said, her voice carrying a hint of sorrow. "To restore harmony, you must endure the Trials of the Elements."

Ling's heart raced with anticipation, knowing that these trials would test their courage, resilience, and connection with nature. He glanced at his companions, seeing determination in their eyes.

Celestia led them deeper into the enchanted forest, where the air grew heavy with a sense of magic. They arrived at a grand clearing where four stone pillars stood tall, each representing a different element - Earth, Wind, Fire, and Water.

Ling approached the pillar of Earth, feeling the coolness of the stone against his palm. A voice echoed in his mind, "To truly understand the earth, you must learn to connect with all living things."

He closed his eyes, focusing his thoughts on the forest surrounding him. Ling felt the gentle vibrations of the forest floor beneath his feet, listening to the whispers of leaves and the songs of birds. At that moment, he realized the interconnectedness of every living creature.

Mei stepped forward, her hand touching the pillar of Wind. The whispering voice urged her, "To harness the wind, you must learn to adapt and embrace change."

With a deep breath, Mei spread her arms wide, feeling the wind brush against her cheeks. She allowed herself to sway, mimicking the graceful dance of the trees. Mei understood that change was a natural part of life, and by embracing it, she could remain resilient.

Sora approached the pillar of Fire, feeling its warmth against her fingertips. The voice within her urged, "To master fire, you must find the strength within yourself to ignite hope."

Closing her eyes, Sora summoned her inner strength, visualizing the flames dancing in her heart. She understood that hope had the power to guide others through the darkest of times, just as fire offered warmth and light in the coldest nights.

Amara stood before the pillar of Water, listening to the soothing voice in her mind. "To flow with water, you must learn to let go and trust in the journey."

Amara took a deep breath and visualized a serene river, bending and curving with ease. She understood that sometimes, the greatest strength came from surrendering control and allowing oneself to be carried by life's currents.

As their trials concluded, a radiant energy connected them all. Celestia smiled, her eyes filled with pride. "You have proven yourselves worthy," she said. "Now, together, you must face the final trial."

Ling, Mei, Sora, Amara, and Celestia followed a winding path, their steps united and resolute. Ahead, they saw a towering mountain, its peak obscured by clouds. The mountain represented the ultimate trial, one that would challenge their every belief and test the strength of their bond.

With their hearts intertwined and determination burning within them, Ling and his companions marched forward, ready to face whatever lay ahead. Little did they know, the true test awaited them at the summit, where their destinies would be shaped and their mission of restoring harmony between humans and nature would reach its climax.

## Chapter 67

Ling, Mei, Sora, and Amara stood side by side, faces etched with determination, ready to face the final trial that would test the strength of their bond. Together, they stepped forward into a dense thicket, their hearts beating with anticipation.

As they pushed their way through the tangled vines, a sudden gust of wind whispered through the trees, rustling the leaves above. The air crackled with an electric energy, sending shivers down their spines. Ling's gaze flickered towards Mei, who nodded in silent reassurance.

Just as they emerged from the thicket, a deafening roar pierced the air, causing them to freeze in their tracks. Before them stood an enormous, fire-breathing dragon, its scales shimmering with a radiant golden light. Ling's wise eyes widened with surprise, his mind racing to comprehend the unexpected turn of events.

"Who dares to disturb the slumber of the Guardian of the Forest?" the dragon bellowed, its voice echoing with power.

Ling took a step forward, his voice steady but respectful. "We are Ling, Mei, Sora, and Amara. We seek to restore harmony between humans and nature."

The dragon's fiery eyes narrowed, studying them intently. "Many have failed this trial before. Are you prepared to face the challenges that lie ahead? Are you willing to sacrifice for the greater good?"

Ling felt a surge of determination coursing through his veins. "We are," he replied, his voice unwavering.

The dragon's gaze softened, a flicker of curiosity dancing in its eyes. "Very well," it rumbled. "To prove yourselves worthy, you must pass through my flames unscathed. Only then will you be granted the knowledge you seek."

Without hesitation, Ling, Mei, Sora, and Amara shared a determined glance before stepping forward, their spirits ablaze with courage. They walked towards the dragon, its fiery breath intensifying with each step.

As the flames erupted around them, Ling closed his eyes and focused on the harmonious energy of the forest. He channeled its power, allowing it to surround him like a protective shield. Mei, Sora, and Amara followed suit, drawing strength from their connections to nature.

Within the inferno, the friends started to dance, their movements fluid and graceful, like flames flickering in the wind. The dragon watched in awe as they weaved through the fire unscathed, their determination unwavering.

With a final burst of energy, Ling, Mei, Sora, and Amara emerged from the flames, victorious. The dragon's eyes glowed brightly as it nodded in approval.

"You have proven yourselves worthy," the dragon declared, its voice resonating with pride. "The knowledge you seek lies deep within the Heart of the Forest, guarded by powerful enchantments. Take this amulet; it will guide you toward your destiny."

The dragon extended its clawed hand, revealing a shimmering amulet adorned with a delicate leaf-shaped pendant. Ling reached out, his fingers wrapping around the amulet, a surge of warmth spreading through his body.

As they bid farewell to the dragon, Ling, Mei, Sora, and Amara felt a newfound sense of purpose. With the amulet as their guide, they ventured deeper into the forest, determined to face the challenges that awaited them.

Little did they know that their encounter with the dragon was just the beginning of their journey. Secrets, mystical creatures, and unforeseen trials would test their resolve, but with the wisdom of Ling, the unwavering spirit of Mei, the boundless curiosity of Sora, and the gentle strength of Amara, they were ready to face whatever lay ahead.

Together, they would push forward, their hearts filled with hope, knowing that even in the face of the unexpected, their bond would guide them toward restoring harmony between humans and nature.

## Chapter 68

As Ling, Mei, Sora, and Amara emerged from the thicket, they felt a gentle breeze brush against their faces. The air seemed lighter, carrying a sense of hope and renewed determination. The amulet glowed softly as if guiding them forward on their path.

They found themselves standing at the edge of a vast meadow, speckled with an array of colorful wildflowers swaying in the breeze. The grass beneath their feet felt soft, like a gentle caress. Ling couldn't help but smile, feeling the weight of their mission slowly lifting from his shoulders.

In the distance, they spotted a shimmering figure. It was a sprite, small in stature but radiating an ethereal glow. The sprite floated towards them, leaving a trail of sparkling dust in its wake.

"Greetings, brave adventurers," the sprite

chimed, her voice tinkling like the sweetest melody. "I am Lumina, the spirit of light. I have been watching over your journey, and I am here to guide you through the final stages of your quest."

Ling, Mei, Sora, and Amara exchanged glances, their hearts filled with gratitude. Their weary souls were in need of Lumina's guidance, a beacon of light in the midst of darkness.

Lumina led them deeper into the meadow, where a towering tree stood at its heart. Its branches reached high into the sky, adorned with countless glowing orbs. Ling recognized it instantly the Tree of Light, rumored to hold the key to restoring harmony between humans and nature.

"Before you approach the Tree of Light," Lumina said, her voice carrying a gentle warning, "you must first embrace the light within yourselves. Only those who possess pure intentions can unlock the tree's true power."

The group studied Lumina's words, understanding the significance of her message. Ling remembered the unity and love that had brought them together, and he felt a renewed sense of purpose.

Each of them stepped forward, their hearts open and their minds clear. Mei closed her eyes and visualized the joy of seeing children playing amidst the trees. Sora imagined a world where wildlife thrived, and humans lived in harmony with nature. Amara pictured clean rivers, free from pollution, reflecting the beauty of the surrounding forests.

Ling, too, let his mind wander, envisioning a future where wisdom and respect guided humanity's path. They felt a warmth emanating from within, spreading through their veins like liquid sunshine. Their bodies glowed with a soft, golden light that harmonized with the flickering orbs of the tree.

A whisper filled the air as the Tree of Light awakened, branches swaying in a dance of celebration. Ling, Mei, Sora, and Amara looked at one another, their spirits lifted by the realization that they were one step closer to fulfilling their mission.

Lumina bestowed upon each of them a small vial containing a radiant liquid from the Tree of Light. "This is the essence of harmony," Lumina explained. "It will guide you further on your quest, and help you overcome any obstacles that lie ahead."

With their spirits renewed, and the essence of harmony coursing through their veins, Ling, Mei, Sora, and Amara stood tall. They were ready for the challenges yet to come, knowing that the light within them would guide their every step.

As they ventured forth from the meadow, the amulet glowed brighter than ever, its vibrant light illuminating the path ahead. They were filled with hope, ready to face whatever trials awaited them, and to restore the harmony between humans and nature that their hearts yearned for.

# Chapter 69

The group of friends, Ling, Mei, Sora, and Amara, continued their journey through the dense forest. They moved cautiously, aware that the next trial would test their unity and resolve. Ling could feel the weight of their mission resting on his small shoulders, but he knew they had come too far to give up now.

As they ventured deeper into the forest, the air grew colder, and the silence became deafening. Ling's heart pounded in his chest, and he glanced at his friends, seeing the determination etched on their faces. They had become a family, bound by their shared purpose.

Suddenly, the ground beneath them trembled, and a deep rumbling echoed through the forest. A massive stone structure emerged from the earth, towering over them. It was the Trial of Strength, a colossal obstacle that tested their physical prowess and teamwork.

Ling swallowed hard, realizing the enormity of the challenge in front of them. He turned to Mei, Sora, and Amara, and when their eyes met, he saw unwavering resolve mirrored in their gazes. Ling knew that they were ready to face whatever lay ahead.

The Trial of Strength required them to scale the treacherous walls of the stone structure, with each level becoming more difficult than the last. Ling took the lead, his nimble fingers finding crevices in the stone to help him ascend. Mei followed closely behind, her determination shining through her every move. Sora and Amara, using their strength and agility, climbed alongside them, their muscles flexing with each powerful stride.

They encouraged one another, never faltering in their determination. Ling found solace in the strength that emanated from his friends, fueling his resolve. Together, they conquered every obstacle, pushing past their limits.

Finally, they reached the summit of the Trial of Strength, breathless but triumphant. Ling turned to admire the breathtaking view, the treetops stretching as far as his eyes could see. He knew that they were one step closer to restoring harmony between humans and nature.

As they caught their breath, a soft voice filled the air. Ling and his friends turned to see Lumina, the spirit of light, standing before them. Her radiant presence filled them with renewed hope.

"Ling, Mei, Sora, and Amara," Lumina's voice echoed gently. "You have proven your strength and unity. But remember, true strength lies not only in physical might but also in compassion and understanding."

Ling nodded, the words resonating deep within him. He realized that their journey was not just about conquering trials but about learning and growing as individuals.

With Lumina's guidance, Ling and his friends descended the stone structure, their hearts filled with determination and newfound wisdom. Each step they took brought them closer to their ultimate goal: to restore the balance between humans and nature.

As they continued their journey, Ling couldn't help but feel a surge of gratitude for the incredible bond he shared with Mei, Sora, and Amara. They had faced numerous challenges, but their unity had never wavered.

Together, they ventured forth, ready to face whatever trials awaited them, knowing that their friendship and unwavering determination would guide them through even the darkest of times. The fate of the forest rested in their hands, and Ling was determined to honor the wise monkey within him and protect their beloved home.

## Chapter 70

The sun shone brightly through the thick canopy of the forest as Ling and his friends pressed onward. Their faces were etched with determination, each step bringing them closer to their ultimate goal of restoring harmony between humans and nature.

As they walked, the forest seemed to come alive with whispers and rustling leaves. Ling's keen instincts told him that they were being watched. He motioned for the group to stop and listened intently, his wise monkey ears picking up on the faint sound of footsteps.

Out from behind the trees emerged a group of creatures, unlike any Ling had ever seen before. They were small, with delicate wings that shimmered in the dappled sunlight. Butterflies! Ling's heart swelled with joy as he realized that the forest had sent them allies in its magical way.

The butterflies flitted around Ling and his friends, their colorful wings leaving trails of iridescent dust in the air. Ling smiled, feeling a connection between the creatures and the ancient stories he had heard about the forest's guardians.

With a graceful flutter, the largest butterfly landed on Ling's outstretched finger. Its wings were a vibrant mixture of blues and purples, reflecting wisdom and serenity. Ling knew that this butterfly held a special message.

"Dear Ling and friends," the butterfly spoke in a melodious voice. "We are the Guardians of the Forest, entrusted with protecting this sacred land. We have seen your bravery and dedication to our cause."

Ling bowed respectfully, his friends following suit. "We are honored to meet you, Guardians," he replied.

The butterfly continued, "The Trials of the Elements have tested your strength, unity, and connection to nature. You have proven yourselves worthy. Now, it is time for the final trial."

Ling's eyes sparkled with anticipation. "What is the nature of this final trial, Guardians?"

The butterfly paused before answering, its voice filled with a mix of gravity and hope. "The final trial is the Trial of Wisdom. It will test your ability to make wise choices, see beyond the surface, and guide others towards harmony.

Only by completing this trial can you truly restore the balance between humans and nature."

Ling nodded, his mind already spinning with thoughts and strategies. He knew that this trial would require more than physical strength; it would require the collective wisdom and knowledge of his friends.

With their newfound allies, Ling and his friends ventured deeper into the forest, ready to face the Trial of Wisdom head on. They knew that whatever challenges awaited them, they would face them with open hearts and sharp minds.

As they walked, Ling could feel the weight of responsibility settle upon his shoulders. He knew that the outcome of this trial would determine not only the fate of their forest sanctuary but also the future of the world outside.

With each step, Ling grew more resolved. He would do whatever it took to protect their beloved home and ensure a future where humans and nature coexist in harmony. The wisdom of the forest flowed through him, guiding his every thought and action.

Amidst the whispers of the trees and the gentle flutter of butterfly wings, Ling and his friends pressed on. The Trial of Wisdom awaited them, and they were ready to prove their worth.

## Chapter 71

Ling and his friends walked deeper into the forest, their hearts filled with anticipation and a hint of nervousness. The Trial of Wisdom awaited them, and they knew they had to be prepared for whatever challenges lay ahead.

As they journeyed, the trees whispered ancient tales of wisdom, their branches swaying in rhythm with the wind. Ling listened attentively, absorbing the words of the forest, as he guided his friends through a maze of towering trees.

Suddenly, a burst of bright light shone through the foliage, illuminating a clearing ahead. Ling and his friends cautiously approached, their eyes widening as they saw what lay before them.

In the center of the clearing stood a massive stone archway, intricately carved with symbols and runes. It seemed to radiate an aura of knowledge and power. Ling's eyes sparkled with curiosity, and he motioned for his friends to come closer.

"Our journey has led us here for a reason," Ling said softly. "This archway holds the key to unlocking the wisdom we seek. But we must approach it with humility and respect."

Mei, Sora, and Amara nodded in agreement, their eyes reflecting determination. They stepped closer to the archway, their hands trembling slightly as they reached out to touch its stone surface.

As their fingertips grazed the ancient carvings, a surge of energy pulsed through their bodies. The symbols on the archway glowed with a soft, ethereal light, revealing a hidden message.

"To gain wisdom, one must first acknowledge their mistakes," Ling read aloud, his voice filled with understanding. "Wisdom comes from learning, growing, and embracing our faults."

Mei, Sora, and Amara exchanged glances, their hearts heavy with the weight of their past actions. They knew they had made mistakes in their quest to protect the forest, but they also understood the importance of forgiveness and growth.

Together, they took a deep breath and stepped through the archway, leaving their doubts and regrets behind. The air shimmered around them, and as they emerged on the other side, they found themselves in a tranquil glade.

In the center of the glade stood a majestic oak tree, its branches stretching towards the heavens. Its leaves rustled with a gentle wisdom that seemed to resonate within Ling and his friends' hearts.

"Welcome, seekers of wisdom," a melodic voice echoed through the glade. "I am Elara, the spirit of knowledge. To prove your understanding, you must answer my riddles."

Ling and his friends exchanged determined glances, ready to face the challenge. Elara's voice continued, her words flowing like a gentle stream.

"Speak without words, hear without ears, and respond without sound. What am I?"

The group pondered the riddle, their brows furrowed in concentration. Ling's eyes brightened as he realized the answer.

"An echo," he said confidently. "An echo speaks without words, is heard without ears, and responds without sound."

Elara's laughter filled the glade, a harmonious melody that echoed through the ancient trees. Ling and his friends knew they had passed the Trial of Wisdom, their understanding shining like a beacon in the forest.

As the laughter faded, the wise spirit spoke one final time. "You have proven yourselves worthy, my young friends. Take with you the wisdom you have gained and continue your quest to restore harmony between humans and nature."

With those parting words, Elara vanished, leaving Ling and his friends standing beneath the wise oak tree. They exchanged smiles of triumph, their hearts filled with a newfound sense of purpose and a thirst for the next adventure that awaited them.

Together, they pressed onward, knowing that they were closer than ever to achieving their goal. Ling, Mei, Sora, and Amara walked hand in hand, their bond growing stronger with each step. And as the forest whispered its secrets around them, they felt a renewed determination to protect and preserve the world they held so dear.

## Chapter 72

In the aftermath of the Trial of Wisdom, Ling and his friends felt a surge of confidence. They knew that each trial brought them closer to their ultimate goal of restoring harmony between humans and nature.

As they pressed on through the forest, a distant rumble reached their ears. The ground began to tremble beneath their feet, causing Mei to stumble. Ling rushed to her side, offering a reassuring smile.

"It's okay, Mei," he said, his voice steady. "We've faced so many challenges together. We can handle whatever comes our way."

Mei nodded, her determination returning. Sora and Amara exchanged glances, their expressions mirroring Ling's confidence. In the face of uncertainty, their bond grew stronger.

Suddenly, the trees ahead rustled with an

unusual force. A massive figure emerged through the foliage, towering over the group. It was a colossal elephant, its eyes filled with sadness and wisdom.

"Greetings, young ones," the elephant spoke, its voice deep and melodic. "I am Raja, the guardian of the forest. I have watched your journey unfold, and I am impressed by your resilience."

Ling bowed respectfully. "Thank you, Raja. We seek to restore the balance between humans and nature. Can you guide us on our path?"

Raja dipped his head, a glint of anticipation in his eyes. "I can, but I must warn you, my purpose is to test your resolve. The Trial of Endurance awaits you."

The friends exchanged glances, their hearts pounding with anticipation. Ling took a deep breath and stepped forward. "We accept the challenge, Raja. We will endure whatever tests you have in store for us."

Raja smiled, his trunk gently reaching out to touch Ling's shoulder. "Very well, young one. Together, we will face the Trial of Endurance."

With Raja leading the way, the group delved

deeper into the forest. The air grew still, and a thick mist enveloped them. Ling could sense a presence, watching, waiting.

They came upon a steep, treacherous climb. The path ahead was filled with narrow ledges and jagged rocks, the mist obscuring their visibility. Each step required unwavering focus and determination.

As they ascended, Ling couldn't help but feel the weariness creep into his bones. Doubt whispered in his ear, urging him to give up. Yet, the unwavering support from his friends propelled him forward.

Mei offered a hand whenever Ling stumbled. Sora and Amara encouraged him with their unwavering faith. Together, they pushed through.

At long last, they reached the pinnacle of the climb, panting and sweating, their bodies aching from the exertion. A breathtaking sight awaited them a magnificent waterfall cascading into a crystal-clear pool.

Raja's voice echoed through the mist. "You have passed the first part of the Trial of Endurance. Now, you must find the hidden path behind the waterfall."

With renewed determination, Ling and his friends waded into the water, feeling a surge of energy as they pushed forward. They emerged on the other side, finding themselves in a hidden grotto illuminated by a soft, ethereal glow.

In the center of the grotto stood a majestic tree, its branches reaching towards the heavens. Ling knew this was no ordinary tree it was the Tree of Resilience, a symbol of endurance and strength.

As they approached the tree, a gentle whisper filled their ears. "Congratulations, young ones. You have proven your endurance, showing the world the strength of your friendship."

Ling's heart swelled with pride as he placed a hand on the tree's bark. "Thank you, Tree of Resilience. We will continue to face any challenge that comes our way, for the sake of our home and all living beings."

The grotto echoed with the sounds of their determination. With the essence of resilience coursing through their veins, Ling and his friends emerged from the Trial of Endurance, ready to face the trials yet to come.

Little did they know that their unity and unwavering spirit would soon be tested like never before. The shadows that had lurked in the periphery were growing stronger, threatening to tear them apart. But Ling and his friends remained steadfast, for they knew that as long as they stood together, they could overcome any darkness that loomed over their world.

And so, with the essence of harmony, wisdom, and resilience pulsing within their souls, Ling and his friends continued their journey, ready to face the next trial that awaited them in the vast wilderness that lay ahead.

## Chapter 73

The group stood in awe before the majestic Tree of Resilience. Its branches reached high into the sky, stretching out like protective arms. Ling could feel the ancient wisdom emanating from the tree as if it held the secrets to overcoming any challenge.

Raja, the wise elephant, gently nudged Ling. "This tree holds the power to strengthen our resolve," he rumbled. "But the Trial of Endurance is not yet complete. We must prove ourselves worthy before it reveals its true potential."

Ling nodded, his eyes determined. "We will persevere," he said, his voice filled with conviction. "Just as this tree stands tall against the wind, we too shall withstand any storm that comes our way."

The group gathered around the Tree of Resilience, joining their hands together in a circle. They closed their eyes, taking in the tranquility that surrounded them. Ling's mind focused, drawing upon the wisdom he had gained from the previous trials.

As if responding to their unity, the tree began to emit a soft, warm glow. Slowly, a series of symbols appeared on the bark, intricate patterns that seemed to twinkle with ancient knowledge. The symbols formed a riddle, a message that only those with true endurance could decipher.

Ling leaned in closer, his eyes scanning the symbols carefully. He furrowed his brow, deep in thought. The riddle seemed complex, challenging their minds to delve deeper.

"The strength of a tree lies within its roots, and the true test of endurance is knowing when to hold firm and when to bend," Raja spoke, his voice steady and wise. "Remember, my friends, endurance is not solely about strength, but also about adaptability."

Ling nodded, his fingers tracing the symbols on the tree. He closed his eyes, allowing his intuition to guide him. Slowly, a thought formed in his mind, a solution that seemed to resonate with the tree's ancient wisdom.

"I think I know the answer," Ling said, his voice filled with certainty. "Endurance lies in finding balance. It is the ability to stand strong when necessary, yet also to be flexible in the face of change."

As the words left Ling's lips, the symbols on the tree began to transform, merging and rearranging themselves. The bark shifted, revealing a hidden path leading deeper into the forest.

The group exchanged excited glances, their spirits uplifted by their triumph. Ling stepped forward, leading the way down the path, his friends following closely behind. They walked in silence, their steps lighter, filled with renewed determination.

The Trial of Endurance had tested their willpower and resilience, but it had also strengthened their bond as a group. Ling knew that the challenges ahead would not be easy, but he had faith in their collective strength.

As they journeyed deeper into the forest, Ling couldn't help but feel a sense of anticipation building within him. They were getting closer to their ultimate goal of restoring harmony between humans and nature. Ling knew that each trial they conquered brought them one step closer to achieving that harmony.

With the Tree of Resilience behind them, Ling and his friends ventured onward, their hearts filled with hope and courage. They were ready to face whatever lay ahead, united in their mission to protect the world they cherished.

## Chapter 74

Ling and his friends walked along the hidden path, their steps filled with anticipation and curiosity. The air felt thick with magic, and every tree whispered secrets as they passed by. Rika, with her enchanting presence, led the way, her eyes gleaming with a mixture of wisdom and excitement.

As they ventured further, the forest grew denser, the canopy above blocking out most of the sunlight. Shafts of golden light occasionally pierced through, illuminating the path ahead. Ling marveled at the beauty surrounding him, the lush greenery and vibrant flowers that painted the forest floor.

But amidst the tranquility, a distant rumble reached their ears. The ground beneath them trembled ever so slightly, causing Ling's friends to exchange worried glances. Ling knew that whatever lay ahead would be no ordinary challenge.

Just as they were about to reach a clearing, the ground gave way beneath Ling's feet. He tumbled into darkness, his heart pounding in his chest. When he finally landed, he realized he wasn't alone. His friends had fallen into the same pit, their expressions a mix of surprise and determination.

Before them stood a towering wall made entirely of thorny vines. It seemed impenetrable, a testament to nature's resilience. Rika's voice cut through the silence, calm yet filled with urgency.

"To pass the Trial of Fortitude, we must find a way to overcome this obstacle together," she said, her words carrying a weight of guidance.

Ling surveyed the wall, searching for any weaknesses, any gaps that they could exploit. The vines twisted and turned, forming a complex network of thorns, seemingly impenetrable. But Ling knew that there was always a way if they were willing to look closely enough.

With a determined expression, Ling approached a section of the wall. He reached out and felt the sharp prick of the thorns against his fingertips. But instead of pulling back, he pushed forward, applying gentle pressure.

To his surprise, the vines shifted, revealing a small opening. Ling motioned for his friends to follow, and one by one, they squeezed through the narrow gap. It was a tight fit, and the thorns grazed their skin, but they pressed on, their resolve unyielding.

As they emerged on the other side, a sense of triumph washed over them. They had overcome the first challenge of the Trial of Fortitude, proving their strength and resilience. Ling glanced back at the wall, realizing that the thorny vines had closed up behind them, erasing any trace of their passage.

Rika smiled, her eyes sparkling with pride. "You have shown great fortitude, my friends. But remember, this is just the beginning. The trials ahead will test your spirit and determination even further."

Ling and his friends shared a silent nod, a silent pact to face whatever challenges lay ahead. They carried within them the wisdom and resilience they had gained, fueled by the purpose they held in their hearts.

The forest whispered its support, the trees swaying gently in the breeze. Ling knew that they were not alone. The forest, their animal allies, and now Rika stood by their side. Together, they would continue their journey, step by step, to restore the harmony between humans and nature.

With renewed courage, Ling led his friends forward, their footsteps echoing with a newfound strength. The path stretched out before them, winding deeper into the heart of the forest, where even greater trials awaited.

And as they walked, Ling couldn't help but feel a surge of gratitude for the extraordinary adventure that had unfolded. Little did he know that the most profound secrets of all awaited them, secrets that would shape their destiny and the destiny of the forest they vowed to protect.

## Chapter 75

Ling and his friends pushed through the dense forest, their eyes wide with wonder. Sunlight filtered through the canopy, casting a magical glow on everything around them. They marveled at the vibrant flowers that bloomed in every color imaginable, the fragrant scent filling their senses.

As they ventured deeper, a melodic humming reached their ears. Ling's heart quickened with excitement. He knew they were getting closer to their destination the Enchanted Grove.

The song grew louder, guiding them through the twists and turns of the forest. Soon, they emerged into a clearing, and their breath caught in their throats.

The Enchanted Grove stood before them, bathed in a soft ethereal light. Trees with branches intertwined formed a grand arch that seemed to touch the sky, shielding a mysterious secret within. Ling's eyes sparkled with anticipation.

The group cautiously stepped forward, their footsteps muffled by a carpet of moss beneath their feet. Ancient symbols etched on the tree trunks glowed softly, illuminating the path before them.

As they approached the center of the grove, a gentle breeze began to whisper secrets in their ears. It told tales of strength and resilience, of harmony and balance. Ling closed his eyes, letting the whispers wash over him, feeling a surge of tranquility and purpose.

Suddenly, a figure materialized from thin air a wise owl named Hikari. His eyes twinkled with wisdom as he greeted the group.

"Welcome, brave travelers," Hikari hooted, his voice soothing yet commanding. "You have passed many trials, but the greatest test awaits you within these sacred grounds."

Ling's heart pounded in anticipation. He looked at his friends, their faces filled with determination and trust. They were ready for whatever challenges lay ahead.

Hikari spread his wings and motioned toward

the shimmering pool at the center of the grove. "To unlock the final trial, you must face your deepest fears and emerge stronger than ever before."

Ling glanced at Rika, whose eyes burned with determination. They had faced countless perils, but this would be their ultimate test. The thought filled Ling with both excitement and trepidation.

One by one, they stepped forward, peering into the reflective pool. In its depths, they saw their fears manifest memories of past failures, the weight of responsibility, and doubts that whispered in their minds.

But Ling knew they couldn't let fear control them. With every ounce of courage within him, he faced his reflection head-on, determined to conquer the doubts that threatened to hold him back.

As the others followed suit, their reflections began to shimmer and transform. The fears melted away like shadows, leaving behind a radiant glow of determination and resilience.

Hikari flapped his wings, his voice tinged with admiration. "You have passed the Trial of Fear, my friends. You have shown unwavering courage and strength. The final trial awaits, and I do not doubt that you will succeed."

Ling's heart swelled with pride. They were closer than ever to protecting their home and restoring harmony to the forest. With hopeful hearts, they took a collective step forward, ready to face the last challenge that awaited them in the Enchanted Grove.

## Chapter 76

Eager to complete the final trial, Ling and his friends stood at the heart of the Enchanted Grove, their reflections shimmering in the still pool before them. With every trial they faced, their bond grew stronger, and their determination burned brighter.

As they watched their reflections, the pool began to ripple. Ling's eyes widened, and he exchanged worried glances with Luna, Raja, and the villagers. Something unexpected was about to happen.

In a flash of light, the pool transformed into a swirling vortex, pulling them into its mystical depths. Ling felt himself being carried away, freefalling through a kaleidoscope of colors and images. Panic gripped him, but he reminded himself to trust in the magic of the forest.

Moments later, Ling and his friends landed softly on solid ground. They found themselves in a breathtaking valley, surrounded by towering mountains and cascading waterfalls. But what truly caught their attention was the presence of other animals animals they had never encountered before.

A majestic phoenix soared gracefully across the sky, its vibrant plumage illuminating the valley. Butterflies, shimmering in every hue imaginable, danced among the flowers. Creatures with iridescent scales and sparkling eyes slithered through the undergrowth. Ling had never seen such wondrous and enchanted beings.

The group stood in awe, their eyes wide with amazement as the animals approached them, one by one. They seemed curious, yet welcoming, as if they had been expecting their arrival.

Ling felt a gentle nudge on his shoulder and turned to find a wise-looking owlperched on a branch beside him. "Greetings, noble travelers," the owl hooted softly. "We have been awaiting your arrival."

Luna, Raja, and the villagers exchanged bewildered glances, unsure of how to respond. Ling stepped forward, his voice steady with curiosity. "Who are you and why were you expecting us?"

The wise owl blinked its large, golden eyes and spoke with a voice as soft as a whisper. "We are the guardians of the Valley of Secrets, an ancient realm hidden within the forest's heart. We have sensed your noble quest to protect the forest and restore harmony."

Ling's heart swelled with hope, realizing that their journey had brought them to a place of great significance. "But how did you know we were coming?"

The owl fluttered its wings and replied, "The forest speaks to us, dear Ling. Its whispers carried your tale of courage and determination. We knew you would be guided here, to unravel the final mystery that will lead you to the ultimate revelation."

Excitement and anticipation bubbled within Ling and his friends. They had come so far and faced countless trials, and now, an even greater revelation awaited them. They were one step closer to accomplishing their mission.

With a newfound resolve, Ling turned to his companions. "Let us embrace this unexpected turn of events and discover what awaits us in the Valley of Secrets. Together, we shall unveil the truths that shall guide us to victory."

The animals of the Valley of Secrets, sensing Ling's determination, greeted the group with warm smiles and nods of encouragement. Ling and his friends felt a surge of energy coursing through their veins as if the very essence of the valley had infused them with purpose.

Hand in hand, they ventured deeper into the enchanted realm, ready to face the final trial and unlock the secrets that would shape their destiny. Ling's heart raced, and with each step, he knew that something extraordinary awaited them. Little did he know that the revelation they were about to uncover would forever alter their perception of the world they thought they knew.

The Valley of Secrets beckoned them forth, promising answers and unveiling the true power that lay within them all.

## Chapter 77

As Ling and his friends emerged from the vortex, they found themselves surrounded by a vibrant and mystical valley. Colors seemed to dance in the air, and the scent of wildflowers filled their nostrils.

A soft voice echoed through the valley, "Welcome, brave souls."

Ling turned to see a figure stepping out from behind a majestic waterfall. The being was tall and slender, with iridescent wings shimmering on their back. Their ethereal presence captivated everyone, and Ling knew instantly that they were in the presence of someone important.

The figure approached Ling and spoke, their voice filled with ancient wisdom. "I am Alia, the Enchanted Keeper. I have been awaiting your arrival."

Ling and his friends exchanged glances, excitement, and curiosity bubbling within them. They had heard tales of the Enchanted Keeper but had never imagined they would meet one.

Alia extended a hand towards Ling. "Come,

wise monkey. I sense great power within you."

Ling cautiously reached out and grasped Alia's hand, feeling a surge of energy flow through him. Memories and visions flashed through his mind, showing him the interconnectedness of all living things and the true potential he possessed.

Alia turned to address the group. "Luna, your gift of communication with plants and animals is a rare and precious one. It is a gift that can unite creatures and restore balance. Embrace it, for your destiny is intertwined with this forest."

Luna's eyes widened, a mix of awe and apprehension. She had always known her gift was special, but hearing it spoken by the Enchanted Keeper made her realize the magnitude of her role.

Alia continued, turning to the others. "And you, brave warriors, each possess unique strengths that will be crucial in the trials to come. Together, you are destined to protect this forest."

With those words, Ling and his friends felt a surge of determination and unity. They no longer doubted their purpose. Ling glanced at each of them, a newfound sense of trust and camaraderie between them.

Alia led them deeper into the enchanted valley, sharing stories of ancient battles fought to protect the forest. The group listened intently, drawing inspiration from the tales of courage and resilience.

As the sun began to set, Alia stopped in front of a colossal tree adorned with shimmering leaves. "This is the Guardian Tree," Alia said, her voice filled with reverence. "Within this tree lies the heart of the forest, the source of its magic and energy."

Ling and his friends stared in awe, feeling the immense power emanating from the Guardian Tree. They could sense that their journey had only just begun and that the trials they would face would test their resolve like never before.

Alia turned to Ling, her eyes glowing with confidence. "Wise monkey, you are the key to unlocking the full potential of the Guardian Tree. Through your connection with nature and your wisdom, you can restore balance and protect this sacred place."

Ling nodded solemnly, knowing that the fate of

the forest rested upon his shoulders. With Alia's guidance and the support of his friends, he knew they could overcome any obstacle that lay ahead.

As the moon rose high in the sky, signaling the start of the next trial, Ling and his friends stood before the Guardian Tree, ready to embark on their most challenging adventure yet. United in purpose and fueled by belief, they prepared to face the darkness that threatened their beloved forest.

Little did they know, a rousing battle lay just beyond the horizon, a clash between good and evil that would test their strength, resilience, and the boundless power of their friendship.

## Chapter 78

Ling and his friends found themselves in awe as they stood in the vibrant and mystical valley, surrounded by wondrous and enchanted animals. Alia, the Enchanted Keeper, smiled warmly at them, her eyes sparkled with ancient wisdom.

"You have finally arrived," Alia said, her voice soft yet commanding. "The forest chose you as its protectors, and your journey has only just begun."

Ling glanced at his friends, their eyes filled with determination and curiosity. Together, they stepped forward, ready to embark on the next chapter of their adventure.

Alia led them through the valley, each step creating a symphony of whispers beneath their feet. Ling marveled at the harmony that echoed through the air, a melody that only the forest's chosen ones could hear.

"There is great darkness looming over the forest," Alia spoke, her voice carrying a tinge of sadness. "The trees are weakening, and the harmony is fading. But fear not, for you possess the power to restore balance."

As they continued walking, Ling noticed the delicate flowers began to bloom along their path, their colors intensifying with each passing moment. It was as if the valley itself responded to their presence, offering a glimpse of hope.

Alia paused near a magnificent waterfall, its cascading waters shimmering with an ethereal glow. "The first trial awaits you," she announced. "To restore the forest's vitality, you must collect the tears of the moonlit lilies that only bloom at midnight."

Ling's friends exchanged glances, their excitement tinged with nervous anticipation. Ling knew they were prepared for the challenges ahead, for they possessed the strength that only true friendship could bring.

With Alia's guidance, they ventured deeper into the valley, their steps cautious yet resolute. The air became thick with otherworldly energy, and Ling could feel the presence of ancient spirits guiding them through the darkness.

They arrived at a moonlit glade, where ethereal lilies swayed gently in the breeze. Their petals, iridescent and pale as moonlight, radiated a soft and alluring glow. Ling and his friends collected the fallen tears, their hearts aching with the weight of the forest's sorrow.

But as they reached for the last tear, a deafening roar echoed through the glade, and shadows emerged from the underbrush with menacing eyes. Ling recognized them as the darkness that plagued their forest, vengeful and relentless.

Without hesitation, Ling's friends formed a protective circle around him, their combined powers pulsating with an unyielding strength. Together, they fought back the darkness, their determination unwavering.

Amid the battle, Ling's eyes met Alia's, and she nodded approvingly. At that moment, he understood the true meaning of their journey - it was not just about saving the forest but discovering their courage and resilience.

Through unity and unwavering spirit, they emerged victorious. The darkness retreated, leaving the moonlit lilies basking in the soft glow of the moon. Ling and his friends stood breathless, their bodies covered in scratches and dirt, but their spirits unbroken.

Alia approached them, a proud smile gracing her lips. "You have proven yourselves," she said. "With each trial you conquer, the forest's strength will be restored, and its harmony will once again resonate throughout the land."

Ling and his friends felt a surge of determination fill their hearts. They knew that their journey was far from over. Together, they would face whatever challenges lay ahead, for the love they held for their beloved home was unwavering.

As they prepared to embark on the next phase of their adventure, Ling couldn't help but feel a newfound sense of purpose, threading its way through every beat of his wise monkey heart.

## Chapter 79

Ling and his friends followed Alia through the vibrant and mystical valley, their hearts filled with a renewed sense of purpose. The path ahead was shrouded in shadows, but they pressed on, guided by the faint whispers of the forest.

As they walked, Ling couldn't help but be in awe of the magical creatures surrounding them. Colorful birds with feathers that shimmered like gemstones flitted through the air, while graceful deer with antlers adorned with flowers grazed peacefully in the meadows. Ling felt a deep connection to these creatures, as if they were all part of a larger tapestry, woven together by nature's magic.

Alia led them to a clearing bathed in soft moonlight, where a group of wise old trees stood. Their branches reached towards the heavens, their leaves whispering ancient secrets.

Ling approached the nearest tree, its bark etched with symbols of forgotten lore.

"Welcome, young ones," a deep, comforting voice resonated from the tree. "We have long awaited your arrival."

Ling and his friends exchanged curious glances, wondering how the trees knew of their purpose.

"We are the Evergreen Council," the voice continued, "the guardians of wisdom and knowledge in this enchanted valley."

"We have been watching over the forest and its inhabitants for generations," another tree added, its voice just as ancient and wise.

Ling stepped forward, his eyes shining with determination. "We have come to restore balance to the weakening forest," he declared. "We seek the strength and wisdom to overcome the darkness that threatens our home."

The council of trees nodded knowingly, their branches rustling with approval. "You have shown great bravery and resilience," the first tree responded. "But the trials ahead will test your true worth."

With those words, the trees began to glow, their energy flowing into Ling and his friends. They felt a surge of power coursing through their veins, their spirits intertwining with the ancient magic of the forest.

Alia placed a reassuring hand on Ling's shoulder. "You are ready, my young friends. The first trial awaits you beyond the veil of mist."

Ling and his friends took a collective breath, their hearts beating with anticipation. They stepped forward, through the ethereal mist, and into the unknown.

They found themselves in a dense thicket, where the air crackled with energy. Before them stood a massive creature, its body covered in shimmering scales. It was the legendary Forest Serpent, a guardian of the ancient woods.

"You seek passage through these woods," the Forest Serpent hissed, its voice echoing through the trees. "But first, you must prove your worth."

Ling and his friends exchanged determined glances, ready to face whatever challenge awaited them. They knew that the fate of their beloved forest rested on their shoulders.

And with that, they plunged into the first trial, their hearts filled with courage and their spirits shining brightly. For they were the chosen ones, destined to protect the forest and restore its fading magic.

## Chapter 80

The air crackled with anticipation as Ling and his friends stood before the Evergreen Council. The wise old trees, their branches adorned with shimmering leaves, nodded in acknowledgment of their presence.

"We have been watching over this forest for centuries," spoke the oldest tree, its voice resonating with wisdom. "It is now time for you to prove your worthiness as the chosen ones."

Ling's heart pounded in his chest. He exchanged determined glances with Rika, Kazuki, and Mei, his loyal companions who stood beside him. They had come so far together, and their bond had only grown stronger since their journey began.

The oldest tree continued, "To restore balance, you must face the Trials of Elemental Unity. Only when you have mastered the elements and united their powers can you vanquish the encroaching darkness."

Ling observed the four paths that stretched out before them, each leading deeper into the heart of the enchanted valley. The paths were adorned with symbols representing the elements earth, water, fire, and air.

"Choose your path wisely," the oldest tree advised. "For each trial will test not only your abilities but also your understanding of the forest's delicate harmony."

With unwavering determination, Ling and his friends chose their respective paths. Ling stepped onto the earth's path, feeling the cool soil beneath his feet. Rika ventured onto the water path, listening to the gentle whispers of the nearby stream. Kazuki embraced the fire path, warmth radiating from the flickering flames that danced along his way. Mei embarked on the air path, her hair fluttering in a breeze only she could sense.

As they ventured deeper into the trials, they encountered obstacles and puzzles that tested their strength, courage, and unity. Ling manipulated the earth with precision, shaping it to overcome each challenge. Rika's connection with water allowed her to navigate treacherous currents effortlessly. Kazuki harnessed the power of fire, igniting his determination to overcome every obstacle. Mei's affinity with the air granted her the ability to soar above hindrances, granting her a bird's-eye view of the trials.

Together, they overcame each trial, supporting one another and relying on their growing bond. The elements responded to their determination, acknowledging them as the true guardians of the forest.

Finally, Ling and his friends arrived at the heart of the enchanted valley, a sacred grove shrouded in a soft, golden glow. Alia stood before them, a smile of pride on her face.

"You have done well," Alia said, her voice filled with admiration. "You have proven yourselves worthy of the forest's trust."

Ling's chest swelled with a mix of pride and relief as Alia continued, "But the journey is not yet over. The darkness grows stronger, threatening to devour the forest. You must now face the ultimate trial and confront the source of this encroaching shadow."

With renewed determination, Ling and his

friends nodded. They were prepared to face whatever stood in their way and protect the forest that had become their home.

As they entered the final stage of their journey, Ling felt the weight of responsibility settles upon his shoulders. The trials had tested their strengths, but the true test of their unity still lay ahead.

With the power of the elements pulsating within them, Ling and his friends stepped forward, ready to face the ultimate trial and fulfill their destiny as the chosen ones; the guardians of the forest.

## Chapter 81

The air crackled with anticipation as Ling and his friends stood at the heart of the enchanted valley. They gazed at the ominous, swirling darkness that loomed before them, knowing that within its depths lay the source of their mission. Alia, the Enchanted Keeper, stood beside them, her ethereal figure radiating a calming energy.

"Beyond this darkness lies the origin of the encroaching shadow," Alia spoke, her voice filled with both caution and hope. "It is there that you will face the ultimate trial and reaffirm your commitment to this sacred duty."

Ling nodded, his heart pounding with a mix of determination and trepidation. He glanced at his friends, each one wearing a resolute expression that mirrored his own. Together, they had relied on their strengths, but now they would need to unite their powers to overcome the impending challenge.

"Remember," Alia continued, her voice steady, "the darkness thrives on fear and doubt. You must trust in yourselves and in the unity you have forged. Only then can you hope to prevail."

Taking a deep breath, Ling and his friends stepped forward, their feet sinking slightly into the soft earth beneath them. As they advanced, the darkness seemed to stretch and deepen, attempting to intimidate them. But they pressed on, refusing to let fear consume them.

As they drew nearer, a series of elemental guardians materialized before them, each representing a different aspect of nature. A fierce firebird flickered into existence, its flames dancing with intensity. A graceful water nymph emerged, her movements fluid and soothing. An ancient earth golem rumbled into view, its moss-covered body emanating strength. And finally, a spirited gust of wind coalesced, swirling with both gentleness and power.

Ling and his friends stood before the guardians, their hearts racing. Each one extended a hand, offering a symbol of their bond and their commitment to protecting the forest. The firebird accepted a small flame, the water nymph cupped a droplet of water, the earth golem held a handful of soil, and the wind spirit gently embraced a wisp of air.

With the elemental guardians satisfied, they dispersed, leaving a path through the darkness illuminated by a soft, pulsating light. Ling and his friends exchanged determined glances and stepped forward, their combined powers resonating within them.

As they ventured deeper into the darkness, their senses heightened. They heard the faint whispers of the forest, felt the pulse of ancient magic, and caught glimpses of their reflections flickering like shadows on the periphery of their vision.

Suddenly, the darkness parted, revealing a cavern bathed in an otherworldly glow. Ling's heart skipped a beat as he beheld what lay before them a massive, twisted tree, its gnarled branches stretching out like grasping hands. Dark energy crackled around it, feeding its malevolent power.

"The Heartwood," Alia whispered, her voice filled with both awe and concern. "It is the nexus of the encroaching darkness. Destroy it, and the forest will be free."

Ling and his friends shared a determined nod, their bond strengthening with each passing moment. They had prepared for this. They had trained and faced countless trials to reach this pivotal moment.

With their combined powers, they launched themselves into battle, their strengths blending seamlessly. Fire clashed with dark energy, water fought against decay, earth held strong against corruption, and wind swept away the tendrils of malevolence.

The battle raged on, each strike resonating with the weight of their commitment. Ling and his friends poured every ounce of their strength and determination into their attacks, refusing to falter. Inch by inch, they pushed back the darkness, their unity forcing it to retreat.

Finally, under the combined assault, the Heartwood trembled. Cracks snaked up its trunk, and a final blast of energy enveloped it, disintegrating the twisted tree into nothingness. The darkness that had plagued the forest dissipated, leaving behind only the gentle sway of restored magic.

Ling and his friends stood amidst the remnants of the conquered darkness, their chests heaving, but their spirits alight with victory. They had faced the ultimate trial and emerged triumphant.

As the forest bathed in newfound light, Ling couldn't help but feel a sense of profound fulfillment. The journey had been arduous, but his purpose had been fulfilled. He and his friends had upheld their duty as guardians of the forest.

But as their elation settled, Ling knew that their journey was far from over. There were still mysteries to unravel, dangers to face, and a world to protect. With newfound determination and unity, Ling and his friends embraced the unknown, ready to face whatever challenges lay ahead, secure in the knowledge that together, they could conquer anything and restore balance to the heart of the forest.

## Chapter 82

Ling and his friends stood amidst the aftermath of their victorious battle, panting heavily. The once malevolent Heartwood now lay in ruins, its dark power dissipated into the air. The forest seemed to breathe a sigh of relief as nature began to reclaim its rightful place.

As Ling surveyed their surroundings, he couldn't help but feel a sense of immense pride. The bond that had formed between him and his friends had grown stronger throughout their trials, and their unity had proven to be an unstoppable force against the encroaching darkness.

Alia approached Ling, a radiant smile adorning her face. "You have done well, young ones," she said, her voice filled with warmth and pride. "You have fulfilled your destiny as the guardians of this forest."

Ling's chest swelled with a mixture of gratitude

and humility. He knew that their journey was far from over, and there was still much work to be done to restore the forest's balance completely. But with his friends by his side, Ling felt an unyielding determination that they could overcome any obstacle that lay ahead.

"We won't stop until this forest is thriving once again," Ling declared, his voice steady and resolute. His friends nodded in agreement, their eyes gleaming with determination.

Alia's wise gaze fell upon Ling, her expression filled with unwavering faith. "Remember, Ling, a wise monkey has the power to not only protect but also inspire. Your courage and determination have already ignited a spark within the hearts of the forest's creatures."

Ling felt a surge of pride at Alia's words. He realized that their journey had not only been about saving the forest but also about inspiring others to find their strength and fight for what they believed in. Ling knew that their triumph over the encroaching darkness would serve as a beacon of hope for all who cherished the natural world.

With their hearts lifted, Ling and his friends turned their attention to their next task:

rebuilding the forest and nurturing its inhabitants. The once vibrant and mystical valley would flourish once more, with Ling and his friends at the forefront of its revival.

As they began their work, Ling couldn't help but feel a profound sense of gratitude for the trust that had been placed upon him. He knew that being a guardian of the forest wasn't just a responsibility, but a privilege. Ling vowed to honor that privilege every day, protecting the forest that had become his home and sharing its wisdom with those who were willing to listen.

And so, Ling the wise monkey and his friends embarked on their new mission, their spirits ablaze with determination and their hearts filled with the knowledge that together, they held the power to make a difference. With every step they took, the forest whispered its gratitude, knowing that its future was in capable hands.

The story of the wise monkey would continue to unfold, intertwining with the lives of those who sought its wisdom and drawing strength from the unity of its protectors. Together, they would ensure that the forest's beauty and magic would endure for generations to come.

## Chapter 83

Ling and his friends basked in the aftermath of their victory, reveling in the newfound harmony that had settled upon the once-encroached forest. The air felt lighter, and the trees swayed with renewed vitality.

As they ventured deeper into the forest, Ling couldn't help but notice a sense of tranquility washing over him. The creatures of the forest, once fearful and wary, now approached the group with curiosity and renewed trust.

The wise monkey's heart swelled with pride as he watched his friends being adored by the woodland creatures. Arturo, the brave deer, stood majestically with his antlers held high, while Kaya, the clever fox, playfully darted through the underbrush, enticing the smaller animals to join her in a game of chase.

Ling knew their victory was not just for the forest but for all the creatures that called it home. He couldn't help but feel a sense of responsibility to protect them, not just from human threats but from any harm that might befall them.

As Ling pondered this, a rustle in the nearby bushes caught his attention. He turned to see a young fawn emerge, its eyes filled with curiosity and innocence. The fawn timidly approached Ling, its tiny hooves stepping carefully on the forest floor.

Ling extended a gentle hand, allowing the fawn to nuzzle against his fingers. He felt a connection, an understanding passing between them. Ling knew that his role as the wise monkey was not limited to protecting the forest from external threats. It also involved nurturing and guiding the younger generations, ensuring a future where harmony and balance could flourish.

With the fawn by his side, Ling led his friends deeper into the forest, guided by an instinctive pull towards an ancient tree standing tall in a sunlit glade. The tree emanated a warm, comforting aura, beckoning them closer.

As they approached, the tree's branches shifted, revealing a hidden path leading underground.

Ling couldn't help but be filled with anticipation. Whatever lay ahead, he knew that he and his friends were ready to face it together.

Descending into the depths, they found themselves in a cavern filled with luminescent mushrooms and glowing crystals. The air was thick with magic, and Ling felt his heart quicken, his senses heightening.

A soft voice echoed through the cavern, resonating with ancient wisdom. "Ling, chosen guardian of the forest," it whispered. "Your trials are not yet over. To truly protect this land, you must confront the darkness within yourself."

Ling's brow furrowed in confusion, unsure of what the voice meant. But he trusted in his journey and, with unwavering determination, prepared himself to face whatever lay before him.

The cavern grew darker, shadows dancing on the walls as a figure materialized before Ling – a reflection of himself, but shrouded in darkness. Ling's heart raced as he recognized this darkness as his fears, doubts, and insecurities.

With each step forward, the darkness seemed to encroach, threatening to consume Ling. But he refused to succumb. He called upon the strength of his animal friends, the lessons he had learned, and the wisdom that resided within him.

As Ling battled the darkness within, his friends watched anxiously, their faith in him unwavering. The cavern filled with echoes of struggle, as Ling faced his inner demons head-on. And finally, with a burst of radiant light, the darkness shattered, leaving Ling standing strong and renewed.

The cavern seemed to exhale, releasing the shadows that had gripped it. Ling emerged, his eyes shining with resilience. He knew now that true strength came not just from defeating external enemies but from conquering the fears that resided within.

With a newfound conviction, Ling turned to his friends, a smile spreading across his face. "We have faced the trials together," he said, his voice filled with determination. "And now, we shall face whatever challenges lie ahead, united in our purpose to protect and nurture this precious forest."

As Ling and his friends ventured forth from the enchanted cavern, they carried with them the lessons learned, the bonds forged, and the unwavering resolve to continue serving as the guardians of the forest.

Little did they know, their journey was far from over. But Ling was confident that with their unity and the strength they had cultivated along the way, they were prepared to face whatever lay ahead. And together, they would ensure that the wisdom of the forest would endure for generations to come.

## Chapter 84

Ling and his friends stood among the vibrant foliage of the rejuvenated forest, their hearts overflowing with joy and gratitude. The creatures of the forest, big and small, had gathered around them with a peculiar glimmer in their eyes. It was as if the animals had something important to convey.

As Ling observed the forest creatures, he couldn't help but notice their strange behavior. Squirrels chatted in hushed tones, rabbits twitched their noses in anticipation, and even the majestic eagles circled above, emitting an aura of eagerness.

"What's going on, my friends?" Ling whispered to a squirrel perched on a tree branch.

The squirrel scurried down, its tiny paws scratching the bark as it approached Ling. "Ling, something extraordinary is happening tonight," the squirrel squeaked excitedly. "The

Animal Elders have summoned all the creatures for a mystical gathering at the sacred clearing. They say it's a rare event that hasn't occurred in centuries."

Intrigued, Ling turned to his friends, their expressions mirroring his curiosity. Without wasting a moment, they followed the squirrel through the forest, the gathering animals creating a harmonious symphony of rustling leaves and buzzing insects.

The sacred clearing greeted them, bathed in the gentle glow of moonlight filtering through the canopy. Animals from all corners of the forest had assembled, their eyes shimmering with anticipation. Ling and his friends took their place at the heart of the gathering, feeling a sense of reverence and wonder fill the air.

In the center, atop a moss-covered rock, stood the wise old owl, revered as the Animal Elder and keeper of ancient knowledge. Its wise eyes bore into Ling's, acknowledging him as the chosen guardian.

"Welcome, Ling, and all esteemed creatures of the forest," the owl hooted, its voice carrying an air of wisdom. "Tonight, we gather to witness an extraordinary phenomenon that occurs only once in a millennium a celestial alignment connecting our world to the spirit realm."

As if on cue, the sky above began to shimmer, revealing a tapestry of vibrant colors and sparkling constellations. The animals gasped in unison.

Ling's heart raced with anticipation as he watched the convergence of celestial energies. Slowly, a translucent bridge materialized, stretching between the spirit realm and their own.

From the other side of the bridge emerged ethereal figures, glowing with a mesmerizing aura. Creatures of mythical tales and legendary beings gracefully crossed over, mesmerizing the forest creatures with their presence.

One by one, they stepped onto the forest floor, weaving their way through the gathering. Dragons with scales of emerald and sapphire, unicorns with golden manes, and fairies with delicate wings fluttered among the animals, blessing them with their touch.

Ling and his friends stood in awe, feeling the weight of this profound encounter. The spirits radiated ancient wisdom and whispered secrets of nature's magic into their ears.

The Animal Elder spoke again, its voice carrying the weight of centuries. "Ling, my young guardian, the spirits have chosen you and your friends to safeguard the forest in its restored glory. The power of unity, love for all creatures, and respect for nature's balance shall guide your path."

Time seemed to stand still as Ling absorbed the wisdom bestowed upon him. He knew that this mystical gathering was not merely a spectacle but a testament to the newfound responsibility he and his friends carried.

With hearts brimming with determination and reverence, Ling and his companions pledged to honor nature, protect the forest, and guide future generations to cherish their connection with the natural world.

As the spirits gradually retreated, the celestial bridge dissipated, leaving only memories etched in the hearts of those present.

Ling and his friends stood united, understanding the significance of the strange occurrence. They were the chosen guardians of the forest, entrusted with a sacred duty to preserve its magnificence for generations to come.

With a renewed sense of purpose, Ling led his friends back into the heart of the forest, their spirits lifted by the mystical gathering. As they walked among the trees, they knew that their journey had only just begun, and new adventures awaited them on the path of their destiny.

## Chapter 85

The morning sun peeked through the vibrant leaves, casting a golden hue on Ling and his friends as they explored the rejuvenated forest. Birds sang melodiously, and a gentle breeze whispered through the trees, carrying the sweet scent of blossoms.

Ling led the group deeper into the heart of the forest, feeling a pull from an unknown source. Their footsteps were light, mingling with the symphony of nature surrounding them. As they ventured deeper, the atmosphere grew mysteriously hushed.

Suddenly, a soft voice echoed through the trees, calling their names in a melodious whisper. Ling's friends looked at each other, their eyes wide with astonishment. Who was calling them?

They followed the enchanting voice, their hearts pounding with anticipation. The sound led them to a magnificent clearing, bathed in a gentle radiance. In the center stood a figure draped in a flowing cloak, their face hidden by a hood.

Ling stepped forward, his voice steady yet filled with curiosity. "Who are you? What brings you to our forest?"

The figure stepped out of the shadows, revealing a woman with sparkling emerald eyes and a gentle smile. "Greetings, guardians of the forest," she said, her voice carrying a soothing melody. "I am Fauna, the protector of all living things. I have watched over this land and sensed the strength and courage within your hearts."

Ling's friends gasped in awe, their gazes fixed upon Fauna. They felt her presence radiating with an ancient wisdom and a profound connection to nature.

Fauna glided toward Ling, her hand outstretched. Ling hesitated for a moment before reaching out and taking her hand. In that instant, he felt an overwhelming surge of energy, as if a connection had formed between them.

"Dear Ling," Fauna whispered, her voice resonating in his mind. "The forest has chosen you and your friends to carry its message far and wide. You have proven your bravery and dedication, and now the time has come for you to embark on your greatest journey yet."

Ling's heart swelled with a mix of excitement and trepidation. He knew that he had a great responsibility resting upon his shoulders. "What must we do, Fauna?" he asked, his voice filled with determination.

Fauna's emerald eyes sparkled. "You must travel beyond the boundaries of this forest to unite all the guardians of nature. Together, you shall confront the looming threat that seeks to destroy harmony and balance in the world."

Ling's friends exchanged glances, their resolve mirrored in each other's eyes. They had come so far together, and they were prepared to face any challenge that lay ahead.

Fauna's voice softened, carrying an air of urgency. "But beware, dear guardians, for darkness lurks in the corners of the world, ready to extinguish the light. Gather your strength, for the journey will be arduous, but remember, united you stand, and together you will prevail."

With those final words, Fauna faded back into the shadows, leaving Ling and his friends standing in the clearing, their hearts brimming with purpose.

Ling turned to his friends, determination glimmering in his eyes. "We have been chosen for a reason," he said with conviction. "Let us honor the trust placed upon us by Fauna and the forest. Together, we shall go forth and safeguard the balance of nature."

His friends nodded, their faces etched with unwavering resolve. They knew that their mission had now expanded beyond the boundaries of their beloved forest. Ling and his friends would journey into the unknown, facing the darkness that threatened their world, guided by the wisdom of the forest and the unyielding bond they shared.

With renewed determination, Ling and his friends set off from the mystical clearing, their hearts filled with hope and their footsteps echoing with purpose. The path ahead would be treacherous, but they were no longer just defenders of their forest. They were now guardians of the world, destined to protect and preserve the fragile balance of nature for generations to come.

## Chapter 86

In their quest to unite all the guardians, Ling, and his friends traversed through dense forests and crossed rushing rivers. Their hearts were filled with determination, and their steps were guided by the whispers of the wind.

As they ventured deeper into the unknown, they stumbled upon an ancient tree, its branches reaching toward the sky like an outstretched hand. Ling sensed a powerful aura emanating from within, and his curiosity led him to approach it cautiously. As his friends gathered around, a voice echoed through the air, gentle yet strong.

"Welcome, young guardians," the voice beckoned, carrying an air of wisdom. "I am Elder Willow, the ancient spirit of this enchanted forest."

Ling felt a surge of excitement and respect. He knew that Elder Willow held the key to unlocking the true potential of their mission. With reverence, Ling stepped forward and spoke, "Elder Willow, we have come seeking your guidance. We wish to unite all the guardians and confront the looming threat that imperils the harmony and balance of our world."

Elder Willow's branches rustled in acknowledgment, and the voice resonated once more. "Ling, you possess the spirit of a true leader in your heart. I have been waiting for your arrival. Uniting the guardians is your destiny, and I will assist you in this noble endeavor."

Ling's friends exchanged glances, their expressions filled with hope and determination. They now knew that their journey had a purpose beyond what they had initially imagined.

Elder Willow continued, "The guardians are scattered across the land, each guarding a specific element of nature. To unite them, you must seek the Island of Elements, a sacred place where they will gather under a full moon."

Ling's excitement grew, and he asked, "But how will we find this sacred island, Elder Willow?"

"Patience, young one," the voice replied. "Only those who possess a pure heart and unwavering dedication can unlock the secrets to the Island of Elements. As you journey forth, remember to embrace the teachings of the forest and trust in the power of your bond."

With those words, Elder Willow's energy enveloped Ling and his friends. They closed their eyes and felt a surge of warmth as if the ancient tree was infusing them with its wisdom.

When they opened their eyes, the sun was beginning to set, casting a golden glow upon the forest. Ling and his friends knew that their path lay ahead, and their hearts were filled with renewed purpose.

"Let us continue our journey," Ling said, his voice filled with determination. "The Island of Elements awaits, and we must fulfill our destiny as guardians of nature."

With a united spirit, Ling and his friends pressed on, their steps now guided by the wisdom bestowed upon them by Elder Willow. They knew that their mission to unite the guardians was no longer just a dream but a tangible reality waiting to unfold.

## Chapter 87

Ling and his friends sailed across the sparkling waters toward the legendary Island of Elements. The wind guided them, whispering ancient secrets in their ears. The island stood tall and majestic, shrouded in a mystical haze that emanated from its core.

As they approached the island, Ling noticed the vibrant colors of swirling energy surrounding it. It felt alive, pulsating with untold power. He knew that this was the place where their journey would reach its pinnacle.

Setting foot on the island, Ling and his friends were greeted by a chorus of gentle voices. The guardians of nature emerged from different parts of the forest, their eyes filled with determination and hope. Ling's heart swelled with pride as he realized how far they had come.

The island seemed to respond to their presence,

its atmosphere crackling with anticipation. Ling led his friends through a lush jungle, where the trees whispered their blessings and the flowers bloomed with vibrant hues.

They walked for what felt like hours until they reached a clearing bathed in ethereal light. Before them stood an ancient stone pedestal, with a carved emblem of intertwined elements at its center. Ling recognized it as the symbol of their destiny.

As they approached the pedestal, it began to glow, beckoning them closer. Ling placed his palm on the emblem, feeling a surge of energy course through his veins, connecting him to the very essence of nature itself.

At that moment, a voice echoed through the clearing, resonating within their hearts. "Guardians of Nature, seekers of wisdom, you have reached the Island of Elements. Here, the elemental powers await, ready to be harnessed for the greater good."

Ling and his friends exchanged glances, a mixture of determination and awe in their eyes. They had come so far, faced countless challenges, and now they stood at the threshold of obtaining unimaginable power.

With reverence, they pledged their commitment to protecting the balance of nature and restoring harmony to the world. Ling knew that their journey was far from over, but they had found the key to fulfilling their destiny.

As the voice faded, the elemental energy surged from the pedestal, swirling around the guardians. Each member of the group felt a unique connection to one of the elements - earth, air, fire, water, or spirit. Their powers awakened an extension of their unwavering resolve.

Ling watched in awe as his friends embraced their newfound abilities. He realized that together, as a united force, they were unstoppable. Ling's heart swelled with gratitude for their unwavering loyalty and friendship.

With the powers of the elements coursing through their veins, Ling and his friends turned their gaze toward the horizon. A new chapter in their journey awaited, one filled with challenges and unknown dangers. But they were no longer afraid.

Hand in hand, they set off towards the

mainland, where darkness loomed and the fate of the world hung in the balance. Ling knew that they were the last hope for restoring harmony, and he was determined to fulfill their sacred duty.

The Island of Elements faded into the distance, but its energy remained within Ling and his friends, a reminder of the strength they possessed. With fiery determination burning in their hearts, they embarked on the next phase of their extraordinary adventure, ready to face whatever lay ahead.

## Chapter 88

Ling and his friends stood on the shores of the Island of Elements, their eyes filled with awe as they gazed upon the vast expanse of the mainland. The wind whispered through the tall grasses, motivating them to press onward to fulfill their sacred duty.

As they set foot on the mainland, a surge of energy coursed through their bodies, their elemental powers pulsating in harmony with the vibrant life around them. Ling's fur ignited with a fiery glow, symbolizing his connection to the element of fire. Ruby, the fearless leopard, shimmered with an ethereal blue aura, embodying the power of water. Juniper, the agile squirrel, radiated a soft green light, embodying the essence of earth. And Luna, the wise owl, sparkled with a gentle breeze, signifying her affinity with air.

With their elemental powers awakened, Ling

and his friends embarked on their journey, guided by an ancient map handed down through generations. The map led them towards a hidden sanctuary deep within the heart of the wilderness, a place where their collective powers would be tested and fortified.

Through dense forests and treacherous terrain, they pressed on, encountering various creatures both great and small. Ling's wisdom guided them through each obstacle, his keen intuition allowing him to decipher the messages woven within nature's fabric.

One night, beneath a starry sky, Ling gathered his friends around a flickering campfire, its glow casting a warm light upon their determined faces. He spoke, his voice filled with conviction, "We are the chosen ones, entrusted with the duty to restore balance and protect the world we hold dear. Though our path may be arduous, the strength of our unity will guide us through any darkness that dares to challenge our purpose."

His words resonated with his companions, their spirits emboldened by his unwavering resolve. With renewed determination, they continued their journey, relying on each other's strengths and unleashing their elemental powers whenever the need arose.

Days turned into weeks, and as they ventured deeper into the heart of the wilderness, they encountered signs of the looming darkness Ling had sensed. The once vibrant forests were now marred by desolation as if nature itself was weeping for the loss it had endured.

Ling's heart sank at the sight, but he knew that succumbing to despair would only fuel the darkness further. Instead, he called upon the power of fire, summoning its essence to ignite hope within his companions' hearts. The flames danced and crackled, illuminating their faces with a newfound determination.

Armed with the unyielding strength of their unity, Ling and his friends pushed forward, their resolve unshaken. They encountered other guardians along the way, individuals who had also heeded the call to protect and restore the world.

With each guardian they met, the bond of their shared purpose grew stronger, their collective powers intertwining like threads in a grand tapestry. And as the darkness loomed ever closer, they knew that their destiny was drawing near.

United in their mission and fueled by the elemental forces within them, Ling and his friends forged ahead, prepared to confront the looming threat. They felt the weight of their duty upon their shoulders, but it only served to strengthen their resolve.

As they continued on their path, Ling knew that the final battle for harmony and balance awaited them. With their elemental powers harnessed and their spirits intertwined, they stood ready to face whatever challenges lay ahead, unwavering in their commitment to protect the world they loved.

And so, Ling and his friends ventured into the unknown, their steps guided by destiny, their hearts filled with hope. The fate of their world now rested in their hands, and they stood ready to unleash the full force of their elemental powers, united as guardians of nature.

## Chapter 89

As Ling and his friends ventured deeper into their mission, the once vibrant world around them seemed to darken. The peaceful melodies of birds were replaced by an eerie silence, and the gentle whispers of the wind turned into haunting whispers that sent shivers down their spines.

The forest, once abundant with life, now appeared barren and desolate. The trees, once tall and majestic, stood withered and fragile. Ling's heart sank as he witnessed the consequences of neglect and destruction. It seemed as though the darkness they had sensed before was now manifesting in front of their very eyes.

Doubt began to creep into Ling's mind. Was their mission worth it? Were they truly capable of restoring the balance they so desperately sought? Ling's eyes searched the faces of his friends, noticing the worry etched on each one. They too felt the weight of the looming threat, their determination waning in the face of uncertainty.

But Ling refused to let doubt consume him. He knew that even in the darkest of times, they had to hold onto hope. Ling mustered his strength and spoke words of reassurance to his companions. He reminded them of the journey they had undertaken, the obstacles they had overcome, and the power that resided within each of them.

Together, they pressed on, and their determination reignited. Ling's monkey heart beat with renewed purpose as he led his friends through the labyrinthine paths of the desolate forest. The shadows seemed to dance around them, whispering secrets and deceit.

As they walked, the ground beneath their feet trembled. Ling looked up to see dark clouds swirling above, blotting out the sunlight. A sense of impending doom filled the air. Ling's grip on his staff tightened, and he urged his friends to hold fast.

Suddenly, a piercing scream shattered the silence, echoing through the forest. Ling's heart raced as they raced towards the source, their elemental powers ready to be unleashed if needed. They emerged into a clearing, and their breath caught in their throats.

A massive creature, dark and menacing, stood before them. Its eyes glowed with an unnatural crimson light, and its snarling visage sent chills down their spines. Ling could feel the malevolence radiating from the creature, threatening to consume everything in its path.

Ling knew that this was the true test they had been preparing for. The final battle that would determine the fate of their world. With unwavering determination, he raised his staff and summoned the collective strength of his friends.

As the battle ensued, bolts of lightning crackled through the sky, flames danced with fury, and the earth trembled beneath their feet. Ling and his friends fought with every ounce of their being, harnessing their elemental powers to ward off the darkness that threatened to consume them.

But even as their powers clashed with the creature, Ling couldn't shake the feeling that this was merely the beginning of a much larger battle. The darkness wasn't limited to this one creature alone. Ling knew that they had to confront the source, the one pulling the strings from the shadows.

As the battle raged on, Ling's determination grew stronger. He would not let darkness prevail. Ling and his friends fought with every ounce of strength they possessed, each strike and spell infused with their unwavering resolve.

And as they stood together, their bodies battered, their spirits unyielding, Ling could feel the tides of destiny shifting. The path ahead may be treacherous, but he knew that as long as they remained united, they could face any darkness that dared to challenge them.

## Chapter 90

Ling and his friends pressed on, their hearts filled with resolve as they faced countless obstacles along their path. The once lush and vibrant land now lay barren, scarred by the greed of those who sought to exploit its resources. Ling knew that their true strength lay not only in their elemental powers but also in their ability to harness their wisdom.

As they traveled further, Kaida shared tales of ancient civilizations and enlightened beings who had walked this land in times long past. Ling listened intently, his mind open to the wisdom that Kaida bestowed upon them. He learned about the delicate balance of nature and how it could be restored through the unity of all living beings.

Their journey led them to the Ruins of Knowledge, a forgotten sanctuary where immense knowledge and ancient secrets were said to be kept. As they entered the crumbling ruins, Ling and his friends felt a surge of anticipation. They were about to be tested, not only in their physical abilities but also in their mental acuity.

The first trial awaited them in a dimly lit chamber, where a riddle was inscribed upon the worn stone walls. "In the darkest hour, light will guide your way. Seek the reflection of truth to overcome the darkness," Ling read aloud, furrowing his brow in deep concentration.

The group stood together, pondering the riddle's meaning. Ling reached deep within himself, trusting his intuition to guide him. Suddenly, he noticed a beam of sunlight streaming through a small opening in the ceiling, casting a radiant glow upon a peculiar mirror.

With a flicker of understanding, Ling walked towards the mirror and gazed at its smooth surface. The reflection revealed another hidden message, etched into the mirror itself. Ling deciphered the message and spoke the words, "Hope shines brightest when united."

As soon as the words left his lips, the room erupted in a blinding light, causing Ling and his friends to shield their eyes. When the light subsided, they found themselves standing in a vast chamber, adorned with ancient scrolls and tomes.

Each member of the group was drawn to a specific book as if guided by an invisible force. Ling's fingers traced the intricate patterns on the cover of the book he had chosen. Opening it, he discovered pages filled with profound wisdom, detailing the harmony between humans and nature.

They delved into their respective books, immersing themselves in the knowledge within. As they absorbed the essence of each word, Ling felt a surge of enlightenment. He now understood the importance of not only restoring the physical world but also mending the broken relationship between humans and nature.

With their minds expanded and hearts ablaze with purpose, Ling and his friends emerged from the Ruins of Knowledge, ready to face the challenges that lay ahead. Armed with their elemental powers and newfound wisdom, they vowed to share the truths they had discovered and restore harmony to their world.

The final battle loomed on the horizon, but Ling knew that their quest was far from over. There were still more lessons to learn, more wisdom to gather, and more allies to unite. With each step, their resolve grew stronger, and Ling was determined to make a difference, not only for his home but for all beings who called this world their own.

As the sun began to set, casting a golden glow over the land, Ling and his friends set off once again, ready to face whatever challenges lay in their path. With unwavering determination, they embarked on their next adventure, eager to bring hope and restoration to their world, one step at a time.

## Chapter 91

Ling and his friends journeyed on, their spirits unyielding, through the desolate land. As they traveled, the air grew heavy with a sense of despair. The once lush forests were replaced by barren wastelands, where the earth's cry for help echoed in the silence.

One day, as they trekked across vast dunes of sand, the scorching sun beating down on them, they spotted a shimmering oasis in the distance. Their hearts soared with hope, knowing that relief from the unforgiving heat was within reach.

With newfound vigor, they quickened their pace, their footsteps kicking up sand in their wake. Closer and closer they ventured until they stood at the oasis's edge, their eyes widening in awe.

The oasis was a paradise untouched by despair. Crystal-clear waters nestled amidst vibrant greenery, and blooming flowers painted the landscape with a kaleidoscope of colors. It was a sight that soothed their weary souls and revived their dwindling spirits.

Ling and his friends waded into the enchanting waters, feeling their weariness wash away. As they immersed themselves, the magic of the oasis seeped into their very beings, showering them with renewed energy and clarity.

Amidst the tranquility of the oasis, they noticed a figure watching them from afar. It was a graceful woman adorned in flowing robes, her eyes twinkling with an otherworldly wisdom.

"Welcome, weary travelers," she greeted them, her voice gentle as a whispering breeze. "I am Aria, the guardian of harmony. I have been awaiting your arrival."

Ling and his friends exchanged curious glances, their hearts beating with anticipation. They sensed that Aria held the answers they had been searching for.

Aria beckoned them to gather around, and they sat in a circle, their senses fully attuned to her every word. She spoke of an ancient prophecy, of a time when darkness would threaten to consume their world entirely, and only those chosen by the elements could restore the delicate balance.

"You are not alone," Aria reassured them. "There are others, like you, who possess the power to restore harmony. Seek the remaining guardians each guarding an elemental realm and unite your powers. Together, you will stand a chance against the encroaching darkness."

Ling's heart swelled with determination. The path ahead seemed challenging, yet he knew he couldn't falter. He looked at his friends, their eyes filled with unwavering resolve.

With gratitude in their hearts, Ling and his friends bid farewell to Aria and the enchanted oasis. They carried newfound hope within them, ready to face the trials that lay ahead.

As they ventured forth, Ling couldn't help but feel a renewed sense of purpose. The world needed them, and they would not rest until harmony was restored.

Little did they know, that the next challenge awaiting them would test their strength, courage, and unity like never before. The darkness loomed closer, and with each step, the stakes grew higher.

But Ling and his friends were determined to face whatever came their way.

## Chapter 92

Ling and his friends pressed onward, their hearts filled with determination. Their next destination was the Forbidden Cave, a place rumored to hold ancient secrets. They knew that gaining access to these secrets would be crucial in their mission to save their world.

As they approached the cave, a sense of foreboding washed over them. The entrance was shrouded in darkness, its jagged mouth beckoning them forward. Ling took a deep breath, reminding himself of the courage he had exhibited thus far. With a flick of his tail, he signaled his friends to follow.

The cave was treacherous, with sharp stalactites jutting from the ceiling and slippery rocks beneath their paws. But Ling's friends trusted him implicitly, knowing that his wisdom would guide them through the darkness.

As they ventured deeper, the air grew heavy,

and the temperature dropped. Strange whispers echoed all around them, causing their fur to stand on end. Ling kept his gaze fixed ahead, refusing to let fear take hold.

At last, they reached a chamber bathed in an eerie, greenish glow. In the center stood a statue of a forgotten guardian, encased in stone. Ling approached the statue, his paw resting lightly on its weathered surface.

Suddenly, the statue came to life, its eyes glowing with a pearl of ancient wisdom. Ling and his friends stood in awe as the guardian's voice echoed through the chamber. "Welcome, seekers of truth. I am Mei, the guardian of knowledge."

Mei revealed that within the cave lay a hidden artifact, the Crystal of Enlightenment. Possessing this crystal would grant immense power and insight. But Mei warned them of the challenges they would face to obtain it.

Ling thanked Mei for her guidance and turned to his friends. "We must persevere," he said, his voice steady and resolute. "The fate of our world rests on our shoulders."

With renewed determination, Ling and his

friends delved deeper into the cave, facing perilous traps and mind-bending puzzles. They relied on their strengths, working together as a harmonious team.

Finally, they reached the chamber where the Crystal of Enlightenment lay suspended in mid-air, radiating a soft, ethereal light. Ling extended his paw, his heart pounding with anticipation, and gently grasped the crystal.

A surge of power coursed through his body, filling him with a deep sense of knowing. Ling turned to his friends, his eyes shining with newfound wisdom. "We are one step closer to restoring balance," he declared. "But our journey is far from over."

As they began their ascent from the Forbidden Cave, Ling, and his friends felt a renewed sense of purpose burning within them. They knew that their encounters with Mei and the Crystal of Enlightenment were only the beginning.

With the crystal in their possession, they were armed with knowledge and power. Ling and his friends were ready to face whatever challenges awaited them on their mission to protect their world and restore harmony.

And so, they set off once more, their paws carrying them toward the next destination on their journey. Ling led his friends through winding paths and treacherous terrains, their spirits unyielding, for they were the guardians of their world, and together, they would overcome any obstacle that stood in their way.

## Chapter 93

Ling and his friends emerged from the depths of the Forbidden Cave, their hearts pounding with a mix of anticipation and trepidation. The Crystal of Enlightenment gleamed in Ling's paw, radiating a soft, ethereal light that filled them with renewed hope. They knew they were one step closer to their goal of restoring harmony to the world.

Following the guidance of the ancient prophecy, Ling led his friends towards the next destination - the Hidden Grove. It was said to be a place of immense beauty and tranquility, a sanctuary untouched by the darkness that had overtaken their world.

As they ventured through the decaying forest, Ling couldn't help but feel a heavy sadness wash over him. The once vibrant fauna now withered and lifeless, the air filled with an eerie silence. The encroaching darkness seemed to suffocate the very essence of their home.

But Ling refused to let despair consume him. He had seen the transformative power of hope and unity, and he knew that they held the key to restoring balance. With every step, his determination grew stronger, fueling his belief in the goodness of their cause.

After what felt like hours of walking, a soft, melodious humming reached their ears. Ling's heart quickened, and a glimmer of excitement shone in his eyes. They were close.

As they pushed through a thick thicket of thorny bushes, a breathtaking sight greeted them. The Hidden Grove materialized before their eyes, a haven of lush greenery and vibrant flowers. The air felt alive with the fragrance of blooming life.

In the center stood a majestic tree, its branches reaching towards the heavens as if seeking solace from the darkness that surrounded them. The leaves shimmered with a golden light, and Ling felt an undeniable pull towards this sacred place.

With gentle steps, Ling and his friends approached the ancient tree. As they drew nearer, a voice, gentle yet wise, reverberated through the grove.

"Welcome, brave seekers," it echoed. "You have journeyed far and faced countless challenges. Your determination is commendable."

The voice belonged to an ethereal figure, a spirit of the forest. With a graceful sway, she descended from the tree, her form bathed in a soft glow. Her eyes sparkled with ancient wisdom, and Ling knew this was a moment of great significance.

"I am Selene, the Guardian of Wisdom," she spoke, her voice a soothing melody. "You seek to restore harmony to this land, and for that, I offer you my guidance."

Ling bowed respectfully, his heart filled with gratitude. "We are honored, Selene," he said. "Please, show us the path towards balance."

Selene smiled gently, her gaze encompassing their group. "To restore harmony, you must first understand the value of empathy," she spoke, her voice carrying a profound weight. "In a world consumed by darkness, finding compassion for all living creatures is the first step towards forging lasting peace."

Her words resonated deeply with Ling and his friends. They had seen the consequences of neglect and destruction, and they knew that empathy held the key to transformative change.

With Selene's guidance, Ling and his friends immersed themselves in the teachings of the Hidden Grove. They learned to listen to the whispers of the wind, to walk in harmony with the creatures of the forest, and to cultivate empathy in their every action.

Days turned into weeks, and under Selene's watchful eye, Ling and his friends grew stronger and wiser. They knew that their journey was far from over, but with each passing day, they became more confident in their ability to face the encroaching darkness.

As they bid farewell to Selene and the Hidden Grove, Ling's heart swelled with gratitude. "Thank you, Selene," he said, his voice filled with determination. "We will carry your wisdom with us and do everything in our power to restore harmony."

With newfound purpose, Ling and his friends embarked on the next leg of their journey, their hearts filled with hope and the promise of a better world. They knew that darkness still lurked, but armed with empathy and wisdom, they were ready to face whatever challenges lay ahead.

The story of the wise monkey would continue, as Ling and his friends ventured forth, their path illuminated by the light of friendship and the unyielding belief in the power of unity.

## Chapter 94

Ling and his friends stood at the edge of the Hidden Grove, marveling at the sanctuary untouched by darkness. The air was heavy with silence as if even nature held its breath in anticipation. But as they stepped forward, a foreboding shadow cast its veil over the once vibrant trees.

Whispers filled the air, their eerie tones sending shivers down their spines. The animals stood close to one another, seeking comfort in the presence of their companions. Ling tightened his grip on the Crystal of Enlightenment, its radiance flickering with uncertainty.

They ventured further into the Hidden Grove, their steps cautious and hearts burdened with the weight of what was to come. The once lush vegetation now appeared wilted and sickly, the flowers drooping and petals falling like tears.

As they pressed on, they encountered twisted

vines, like sinister arms reaching out to ensnare them. Ling swung his staff, severing the tendrils with swift and precise strikes. Kaida fought alongside him, her talons slashing through the thick foliage.

But with each step, the darkness grew more oppressive, suffocating the very essence of the grove. The animals' eyes glowed with fear, their instincts screaming of imminent danger. Ling could feel their unease, the harmony they had once embraced was now threatened by an encroaching malevolence.

In the heart of the grove, they discovered a corrupted pool, once a source of life and purity. Now, its once-clear waters turned murky, emitting an unsettling energy. Ling approached cautiously and dipped a finger into the tainted liquid. A surge of darkness coursed through his veins, whispering tempting promises of power.

With a resolute determination, Ling withdrew his hand, resisting the allure. This was not the path they had chosen. He looked at his friends, their unwavering loyalty reflected in their determined gazes.

"Our task is to restore harmony," Ling reminded them, his voice steady despite the apprehension that gnawed at his heart. "We must confront the darkness that threatens to consume this world."

Together, they pressed onward, weaving through the twisted paths of the Hidden Grove. Each obstacle they encountered grew more treacherous, each whisper more insidious. But Ling and his friends did not falter. They found strength in one another, drawing from the well of unity that had guided them thus far.

Finally, they reached the heart of the grove, where an ancient tree stood, its bark gnarled and its branches reaching for the starless sky. The whispers grew louder, their words venomous and filled with malice. Ling raised the Crystal of Enlightenment high above his head, its glow cutting through the darkness.

With a burst of blinding light, the corrupted tree shrieked in agony, its shadowy aura recoiling from the crystal's brilliance. The darkness fought back, wrapping around Ling's friends, trying to pull them away. But Ling stood firm, channeling the wisdom and strength he had gained throughout their journey.

The battle raged, light against darkness,

harmony against chaos. Ling and his friends fought with every ounce of their being, their determination unwavering. As the clash reached its peak, a deafening roar pierced the air, signaling a turning point in the battle between good and evil.

But would Ling and his friends prevail? Would they be able to overcome the darkness that threatened to consume their world? Only time would tell as they pushed forward, ready to face whatever awaited them on the path to restoration.

## Chapter 95

Ling and his friends stood at the edge of the Hidden Grove, their hearts filled with determination. The once vibrant sanctuary now lay shrouded in darkness, its beauty tainted by the encroaching evil. They knew that the path ahead would not be easy, but they were ready to face whatever challenges awaited them.

As they ventured deeper into the darkness, a sense of unease settled upon them. Ling's keen senses picked up on the faint whispers, twisted and sinister as if the shadows themselves were taunting them. But Ling's resolve remained unshaken, and he pushed forward, leading his friends through the gloom.

Suddenly, a voice echoed through the stillness. "Who dares enter this sacred domain?"

Ling recognized the voice as belonging to the Guardian of Serenity, a powerful figure known for her wisdom and tranquility. He stepped forward, his heart pounding, and replied, "It is I, Ling, the wise monkey. I have come with my friends to restore harmony to our world."

The darkness shifted, and a figure emerged from the shadows. A woman, dressed in flowing robes, with a serene expression on her face. "Ling, I have been expecting you," she said, her voice soothing like a gentle breeze. "You and your companions have shown great courage to come this far. But the path ahead is treacherous."

Ling nodded, his eyes filled with determination. "We understand the challenges we will face, Guardian of Serenity. But we are united in our purpose and will not falter."

The guardian smiled, her presence radiating calmness. "Very well, Ling. To restore harmony, you must first find the Key of Serenity, hidden deep within the heart of the Forgotten Forest. It is guarded fiercely by the spirits of those who have lost their way."

With a nod of gratitude, Ling and his friends set out on their new quest. The Forgotten Forest lay before them, its ancient trees whispering haunting melodies that tugged at their hearts. The air grew heavy with an eerie silence as they entered its depths, the once vibrant foliage now coated in a ghostly mist.

As they ventured deeper into the forest, they encountered restless spirits and lost souls trapped in the darkness. Ling understood their pain and sorrow, reaching out with empathy and compassion. One by one, the spirits were soothed, their anguished cries replaced with peaceful sighs as they found solace.

Through countless trials and tribulations, Ling and his friends pressed on, their bond growing stronger with each passing obstacle. Finally, after what felt like an eternity of struggle, they stumbled upon a hidden glade bathed in a soft, ethereal light.

At the center stood a magnificent tree, its branches stretching towards the heavens. Nestled within its roots was the Key of Serenity, shimmering with an otherworldly glow. Ling stepped forward and gently plucked it, a surge of tranquility washing over him.

As he held the key, Ling knew that their journey was far from over. But with the Key of Serenity in their possession, they possessed the means to unlock the next chapter in their quest for harmony.

With newfound determination, Ling and his friends left the Forgotten Forest, their hearts filled with hope. The path ahead would be challenging, but they were ready to face whatever lay in wait. For they knew that the restoration of harmony was within their reach, and they would not rest until their world was once again bathed in serenity.

## Chapter 96

Ling and his friends marched through the Forgotten Forest, their footsteps soft against the lush undergrowth. The air was heavy with anticipation as they followed the map provided by the Guardian of Serenity. With every step, Ling could sense the lingering presence of the darkness that had plagued their beloved forest.

As they ventured deeper into the forest, the atmosphere grew heavier. Shadows danced among the trees, whispering ominous warnings in the wind. Ling's friends huddled close, seeking comfort in each other's company. But Ling knew that they couldn't let fear consume them. They had a mission to complete.

Guided by their unwavering determination, they pressed on, their eyes scanning the surroundings for any sign of the key. The Forgotten Forest was as enchanting as it was treacherous, with towering trees that seemed to reach the heavens and a carpet of moss that cushioned their every footfall.

Ling's keen senses picked up on a faint shimmer amidst the branches. He raised a hand, signaling his friends to halt. They all gazed up, their eyes widening in awe. High above, nestled among the highest branches, hung the Key of Serenity.

It was suspended by delicate chains, glinting with a soft golden hue that pulsed with an ethereal light. But the path to the key was fraught with danger. Ling knew that they would have to face a series of trials before they could claim it as their own.

With unwavering determination, Ling and his friends devised a plan. They split into groups, each assigned to a different trial. Ling took the lead, his instincts guiding him through the maze of twisted roots and hidden traps.

One by one, they overcame each obstacle, fueled by their unwavering resolve and their belief in the power of unity. Ling's heart swelled with pride as he watched his friends conquer their fears and grow stronger with every trial.

Finally, they stood before the Key of Serenity. Its glow reflected in their eyes, casting a serene light over the once-dreary forest. Ling reached out, his hand trembling with anticipation, and gently touched the key.

As his fingers made contact, a wave of tranquility washed over Ling, spreading through his veins like a soothing melody. He could sense the dormant power awakening within him, resonating with the forest's heartbeat.

Ling turned to his friends, their eyes reflecting the same sense of purpose and determination. Together, they unlocked a new level of harmony and strength. Ling knew that their journey was far from over, but they were prepared to face whatever lay ahead.

With the Key of Serenity in their possession, Ling and his friends continued their quest to restore balance to the forest. As they left the Forgotten Forest behind, a sense of hope ignited in their hearts, propelling them forward toward the final confrontation with the darkness that threatened their world.

The journey had tested their mettle, but it had also forged unbreakable bonds of friendship and resilience. Ling knew that with their newfound unity and the power of the key, they were an unstoppable force.

With unwavering determination, Ling and his friends stepped out of the Forgotten Forest, ready to face the challenges that awaited them and restore the harmony that had been lost. The stakes were higher than ever, but they knew deep down that their actions would shape the future of the forest and all who called it home.

## Chapter 97

In the wake of their triumph in the Forgotten Forest, Ling and his friends emerged with a renewed sense of purpose. The Key of Serenity glistened in their hands, a symbol of their unwavering determination. They knew that their journey was far from over, but they were ready to face whatever challenges lay ahead.

With the guidance of the Guardian of Serenity, Ling and his friends set off towards the Shadowed Mountains. The path grew treacherous and steep, but they pressed on, fueled by their shared desire to restore harmony to their world.

As they ascended the mountains, the air grew colder, and a thick fog enveloped them. Ling could sense a growing presence of darkness, lurking just beyond their sight. He tightened his grip on the key, finding solace in its warmth. The journey had tested their resolve, but they knew that the true test was yet to come.

Suddenly, a chilling breeze swept through the air, carrying with it whispers of despair. Ling's friends shivered, their faces etched with worry. But Ling, the wise monkey, remained focused and steadfast. He knew that their mission was greater than their fears.

With every step, the darkness seemed to intensify. Shadows danced in the corners of their vision, threatening to consume them. Yet, Ling refused to succumb to the lure of fear. He had seen firsthand the power of unity and belief, and he was determined to stay true to their purpose.

As they reached the summit of the Shadowed Mountains, the fog began to disperse, revealing a desolate landscape. The once vibrant and lush land now appeared barren and lifeless. Ling's heart sank as he surveyed the destruction that the darkness had wrought.

But he refused to let despair take hold. Ling's unwavering resolve ignited a fire within the hearts of his friends. They, too, refused to succumb to hopelessness. Together, they vowed to push forward, to bring light to the darkest corners of their world.

With the Key of Serenity leading the way, Ling and his friends descended into the heart of the shadowed valley. The air grew heavy with a palpable sense of malevolence. Ling urged his companions to stay strong, to trust in their purpose, and to remember the power of hope.

As they delved deeper into the darkness, they encountered twisted creatures, born of the shadows themselves. Ling and his friends fought valiantly, channeling their newfound strength and unity. They refused to let the darkness extinguish their light.

Finally, at the deepest part of the shadowed valley, they discovered the entrance to the Cave of Ancients. Ling's heart raced with anticipation as he pushed open the heavy stone doors. The darkness within was suffocating, but they stepped forward, guided by an indomitable spirit.

The cave was vast and labyrinthine, its walls adorned with ancient symbols and forgotten wisdom. Ling led his friends deeper into the depths, their determination unwavering. They knew that within the cave lay the answers they sought, the key to restoring harmony to their world.

As they ventured further, Ling's eyes fell upon a faint glimmer of light. His heart leaped with excitement as he followed the glow, leading them to a chamber bathed in ethereal radiance. Before them stood a statue, its eyes gleaming with an otherworldly luminescence.

The statue spoke, its voice echoing through the chamber, "To restore harmony, you must face the darkness within yourselves."

Ling and his friends exchanged determined glances. They knew that the greatest battle lay not in the external world, but within their hearts. With newfound courage, they vowed to confront their fears, their doubts, and their darkness.

Ready to embark on this introspective journey, Ling and his friends gathered around the statue. As they closed their eyes, a surge of energy enveloped them, transporting them into the depths of their souls.

And so, the next part of their quest began to confront the darkness within, to find the strength to overcome, and to emerge as beacons of light in a world consumed by shadow. Ling and his friends were ready to face their inner demons and embrace the power of self-discovery.

## Chapter 98

Ling and his friends stood before the entrance of the Cave of Ancients, their hearts pounding with anticipation. The cave's mouth yawned open, revealing a chilling darkness that seemed to mock their determination. Ling glanced at his companions, their wide eyes reflecting his uncertainty.

"We've come this far, my friends," Ling spoke softly, his voice steady. "We must confront the darkness within us to find the light that will guide us."

With a deep breath, they stepped into the foreboding cave. The air grew colder, the blackness enveloping them like a suffocating embrace. Shadows danced around, whispering secrets and fears. Ling clutched the Key of Serenity tightly, its cool touch reassuring against his palm.

As they ventured deeper into the cave, their

footsteps echoed ominously, resonating with their innermost doubts. Ling's heart clenched, but he refused to let fear consume him. He had guided his friends this far, protecting the forest and overcoming countless obstacles. He would not falter now.

Soon, they reached a chamber bathed in a faint, ethereal glow. The sounds of running water echoed within, filling the cavern with a soothing melody. Ling's eyes widened in awe as he beheld a shimmering waterfall cascading down a crystalline structure, creating a sparkling pool at its base.

"This is the Pool of Reflection," Ling whispered, unable to tear his gaze away from its captivating beauty. "Here, we will face our inner demons and find the strength to triumph."

One by one, they stepped forward, their reflections rippling across the pool's surface. Ling stared at his reflection, his eyes searching for the courage he knew lay within. Shadows swirled, distorting his image, and revealing fears and doubts that threatened to consume him.

Taking a deep breath, Ling closed his eyes, grounding himself in the present moment. He remembered the forest, the animals, and his friends who relied on his wisdom. Slowly, he let go of his doubts and embraced his purpose to restore harmony and protect his home.

As Ling opened his eyes, his reflection in the Pool of Reflection shimmered with newfound determination. The doubts that had once clouded his mind were replaced by a fierce resolve, burning like a flame within him. He knew he had found his inner light.

One by one, Ling's companions followed suit, facing their reflections, and confronting their demons. The darkness within them seemed to wither and fade, replaced by clarity and strength. Ling felt a bond strengthen between them, their unity growing unbreakable.

Together, they stepped away from the Pool of Reflection and continued their journey through the Cave of Ancients. The path twisted and turned, but Ling led them with unwavering faith, guided by the light that now shone brightly within him.

As they rounded a corner, a blinding light pierced through the darkness, signaling the end of their treacherous path. Ling and his friends emerged from the cave, squinting against the sudden brilliance.

Before them lay a vast expanse of flowering meadows, stretching as far as the eye could see. The scent of wildflowers filled the air, lifting their spirits with a renewed sense of hope. Ling felt a profound sense of gratitude, knowing that they were one step closer to restoring harmony to their world.

Gathering their strength, Ling and his friends began their descent from the Shadowed Mountains. They knew that more challenges awaited them, but with the light of their inner resolve guiding their way, they were confident that they could face whatever lay ahead.

And so, Ling and his companions continued their journey, bound together by their shared purpose and unwavering determination. Little did they know, the final trial awaited them a test of their willpower and the sacrifice they were willing to make to restore harmony to their beloved forest.

## Chapter 99

Ling and his friends continued their journey, their footsteps echoing through the vast expanse of the Shadowed Mountains. As they trekked, the air grew colder, and the darkness became more palpable, encircling them like a suffocating blanket. Ling's heart pounded in his chest, afraid that they might lose their way or succumb to the growing despair.

Just as hope began to waver, a faint melody reached their ears. Ling, his eyes widening, motioned for his friends to follow the sound. They navigated through the winding paths until they stumbled upon a hidden oasis, bathed in ethereal light that seemed to chase away the shadows.

In the center of the oasis stood a magnificent tree, its branches reaching towards the heavens. Ling's eyes widened in astonishment as he noticed the tree's lustrous leaves shimmering in all the colors of the rainbow. It was a sight, unlike anything they had ever seen before, a beacon of hope amid darkness.

As they approached, Ling couldn't help but feel a surge of tranquility washing over him. The melodies grew louder, and the tree seemed to respond, swaying gently in response to the rhythm. Ling and his friends exchanged glances, reflecting their shared awe and wonder.

Without warning, the tree emitted a soft glow, revealing a hidden path beneath its roots. Ling's heart raced with anticipation this unexpected turn of events both surprised and intrigued him. The path seemed to lead somewhere significant, perhaps to the answers they sought.

Guided by their newfound curiosity, Ling and his companions descended into the depths of the hidden passage. Despite the darkness enfolding them once more, they pressed forward, their footsteps becoming resolute. The air grew heavy with mystery, and Ling couldn't shake the feeling that they were being drawn into something greater than themselves.

As they ventured deeper, the passage widened, revealing an awe-inspiring sight. Before them stood a vast chamber, adorned with breathtaking tapestries, each telling a different story. Ling's eyes roamed over the intricate threads, captivated by the tales woven into the fabric.

In the center of the chamber, a lone figure materialized a mystical being adorned in flowing robes, their face hidden beneath a hood. Ling and his friends exchanged cautious glances, unsure of what to expect. The figure raised a hand, beckoning them closer.

With a mix of trepidation and excitement, they approached the enigmatic figure. As they drew near, the hooded being spoke, their voice filled with wisdom and ancient knowledge.

"Ling, chosen protector of the forest, you and your friends have journeyed far to restore harmony," the figure began. "But ahead lies the most crucial task where your true strength and purpose shall be tested."

Ling's heart skipped a beat. What could lie ahead that was more challenging than everything they had faced before? Ling and his friends listened intently, ready to face whatever trials awaited them. Their journey had already been filled with surprises, and they knew that this unexpected encounter would only mark the beginning of their greatest challenge yet.

## Chapter 100

In the presence of the magnificent tree, Ling and his friends felt a surge of energy and determination. They knew that their journey had led them to this moment, the final test that would determine the fate of their world.

As they approached the tree, its branches swayed gently, as if beckoning them closer. Ling stepped forward, his heart pounding with a mix of excitement and apprehension. He knew that this test would challenge him like never before.

The tree spoke, its voice resonating through the oasis. "Ling, wise monkey, you and your companions have proven your bond with nature. But now, you must prove your understanding of the delicate balance that exists within it."

Ling nodded, taking a deep breath to steady himself. He knew that his words and actions at this moment would have a profound impact on the future of their world. With every sentence he spoke, he needed to choose wisely.

"As caretakers of this world," Ling began, his voice steady, "we must respect nature and all its inhabitants. We should strive to live in harmony, understanding that every creature has a role to play."

The tree rustled its leaves, seemingly pleased with Ling's response. "You speak truth, wise monkey," it said. "But there is one final challenge you must face before harmony can be restored."

Ling's friends stood beside him, their eyes filled with determination. They knew that whatever lay ahead, they would face it together.

The ground beneath them shifted, and from the depths of the oasis rose a colossal creature, its shadow looming over them. It was a representation of the darkness that had consumed their world, a physical manifestation of the disharmony that had taken hold.

Ling and his friends stood their ground, ready to confront the embodiment of the darkness. They knew that defeating it would require more than just physical strength; it would require unity, compassion, and unwavering belief in their quest.

Together, they fought against the creature, their hearts aflame with purpose. With every strike, they infused their energy with the essence of harmony, pushing back the darkness bit by bit.

Finally, after what felt like an eternity, the creature let out a roar of defeat. Its shadowy form dispersed, dissipating into the wind. The darkness that had plagued their world was no more.

As the oasis transformed into a vibrant haven, Ling and his friends collapsed to the ground, exhausted but triumphant. They had succeeded in their mission to restore harmony to their world.

The wise monkey looked at his companions, a smile spreading across his face. "We did it," he whispered. "We have brought balance and peace back to our home."

With renewed hope, Ling and his friends returned to their beloved forest, spreading the message of harmony and unity to all they encountered. They knew that their journey was just the beginning a foundation upon which their world could heal and flourish.

**And so, the wise monkey and his companions lived out their days, guiding future generations to respect and protect nature. Ling's legacy endured, ensuring that the wisdom he had gained would be shared with all who sought a harmonious existence.**

**In the end, it was the collective efforts of those who understood the delicate balance of nature that saved their world a testament to the power of unity and the indomitable spirit of the wise monkey, Ling.**

Did you love *The wise monkey*? Then you should read *Lovers of dark humour* by Hash Blink and Thomas Sheriff!

Shadows Lurking: A Journey Through Darkness and Light

Immerse yourself in a heart-stopping narrative that defies the boundaries between dark humor and chilling terror. Our tale follows Samuel, a man with an affinity for the macabre, as he discovers a community that initially seems to echo his unconventional passions. Yet, what begins as a shared love for dark humor swiftly spirals into a haunting odyssey of survival and betrayal.

Dive into the Abyss

Samuel's journey propels him into the arms of a clandestine group known as the "Lovers of Dark Humor." Their explorations of humor's outer fringes are thrilling—until a sinister plot unfolds within the decrepit walls of an abandoned mental asylum. Here, Samuel's laughter is choked by fear, and the true nature of darkness is unveiled.

A Quest for Redemption

The tension escalates as Samuel, betrayed and ensnared in a web of psychopathy, seeks escape not just from his former confidants but from the very essence of terror itself. Allies morph into adversaries, and salvation comes from the unlikeliest of guardians—a creature with glowing red eyes that Samuel once feared.

An Unlikely Alliance

As the story evolves, so does the complexity of Samuel's companions. A werewolf with shared grievances offers both protection and a glimpse into a realm where enemies can become allies. Together, they face the Keepers of the Dark, a sect devoted to enveloping the world in eternal night. Through haunted forests, decrepit amusement parks, and battles fraught with peril, Samuel finds strength in unity and a flickering hope that darkness can be overcome.

Embrace the Journey Within Shadows Lurking is not merely a tale of external confrontations; it is an introspective odyssey. Samuel's quest is as much about battling the external embodiments of darkness as it is about confronting his own inner demons. The narrative weaves a rich tapestry of terror and triumph, shadow and light, testing the limits of human endurance and the power of relentless hope.

Prepare yourself for a narrative that transcends mere scares to explore profound themes of humanity, redemption, and the indomitable spirit to fight against impending darkness. Will Samuel and his cadre of unlikely heroes emerge victorious, or will they succumb to the creeping shadows? The answers lie within these pages, beckoning you to explore the threshold between light and utter darkness.

Embark on this exhilarating journey, where every chapter promises to grip your imagination and challenge your perceptions of courage and fear. Shadows Lurking awaits your daring plunge into its depths.

# Also by Hash Blink

The wise monkey

# Also by Thomas Sheriff

The wise monkey

# About the Author

born Thomas B. Sherriff, is a hip hop artist and storyteller. With a global perspective shaped by his Liberian roots and his experiences in the vibrant hip-hop scene of Chicago, Hash Blink's music and literature transcend boundaries and captivate audiences. his captivating narratives. With a passion for exploring the intricacies of human emotion and experience, Sherriff's stories span various genres and offer readers a unique and immersive reading experience.